THE HALETHORPE CHRONICLES

THE ART OF A CURSE

ALY ANDERS

THE ART OF A CURSE

ALY ANDERS

Cover Art by Aly Anders

Cover & Chapter Header Font: Joker by Perfectype

(letterserif.151@gmail.com)

https://www.creativefabrica.com/designer/perfectype

Used under Commercial License

Print Font: Crimson Text by Sebastian Kosch

Used under OFL (Open Font License)

eBook ISBN: 979-8-9916471-5-1

Paperback ISBN: 979-8-9916471-6-8

First Edition

This one is for...
No, this one is for *me*.

The Art of a Curse

This book contains sexual subject matters.
On the surface, it's about falling in lust with a revenant.
But—it runs just a little deeper than that.

Also, I believe that regal ghosts and seductive specters like
Ronan Arslane desire to have their bodies described as if
Shakespeare had written their entire existence.

So, let's ride the shadows and call it prose.
Or poetry.
A prayer perfectly placed.

This book contains scenes depicting domestic violence.
Wren is a survivor of an abusive relationship. Some chapters are
very dense and reveal her memories and mindset during that time.
I understand this may be triggering for some, and I urge you to
decide if Wren's story adds value to *your* healing journey.

If you or someone you know needs help:
The National Domestic Violence Hotline [www.thehotline.org]
can help.
You are not alone.

♫ "Can't Pretend" – Tom Odell

CHAPTER 1

Fresh Start

"Well, it could be worse," I muttered as I pushed open the massive arched oak door to the house. It creaked with years of pain from having gone unoiled and cared for. The space revealed itself— a foyer and living room caught between grandeur and disrepair. The intricate hardwood floors stretched beneath the high vaulted ceilings, and their ornate moldings showed their details in the bright light that came in through the massive windows.

A pink highlighter colored paper fluttered to the floor in front of me. It must have been crammed into the frame.

"Art Auction – Downtown – 7 pm"
RARE ART, HISTORIC PIECES

"Hm," the sound echoed through the room. Today. I committed it to memory, crumpled the paper, shoved it into my bag, and slowly stepped the rest of the way into the foyer in awe and, well, *horror.*

"Home sweet home," I whispered to myself, and the few rodents I'd imagined were squatting *somewhere* close by, judging by the faint smell of must and urine.

This was supposed to be a fresh start, but I felt that perhaps it was *just* a start. The cobwebs hanging delicately from the corners of the room indicated that nothing was fresh about this place.

This was certainly not the sleek apartment I'd left behind in the city—it was old, maybe even ancient by my standards, but it had a charm that tugged at me when I saw the photos.

I bought an old, probably *haunted*, house sight unseen to escape the tattered reality that my life had quickly solidified into chaos and bullshit. I didn't have much time to think about where I'd end up... I just *ran.*

There's something whimsical about starting your day and not knowing your destination. And now, I stood in the center of my consequences—face to face with the culmination of my decisions— surrounded by the bright white that had been painted over whatever history once existed here—**a metaphor for my life.**

Was this room the spectacle, or was I?

How had my life detoured so far from what I'd imagined it to be at thirty years old? Was it the years of failed relationships and subsequent decisions that turned bad far too quickly? Was it years of unhealed childhood trauma?

I stood in the stale air of this grand room, recognizing it for what it was. The start of something *new.* No more sterile apartments with no personality, no more unfulfilling friendships with fake friends, and no more men that made me feel emptier than this room. I didn't have to worry about anyone here recognizing my face from the papers. This place was *nowhere*, and now nowhere was mine.

My phone buzzed in my pocket, snapping me back to the moment. *Sam.*

> **Sam:** Haunted, yet?
> *I smiled, tapping out a reply.*
> **Me:** Not yet. But give me a day or two.
> **Sam:** If the house starts talking...
> **Sam:** Run.
> **Sam:** Don't investigate.
> **Sam:** Just run.
> **Me:** lol hear me out?
> **Sam:** You right. Raw, next question.

Sam always knew how to make me laugh, even from hundreds of miles away. He'd been my rock through some of the more difficult moments in my life. And there were too many of them for me to count. Too many times, I'd sat across from him, tears falling from my eyes and worries drowned under a sea of wine.

We met during our freshman year of high school. Sam was my first boyfriend—and *almost* my first kiss, except he figured out rather quickly that I wasn't his type. We went our separate ways *romantically* but have been best friends ever since. Fate knew what they were doing when they crossed our stars. I only wished they'd spared me the adolescent embarrassment of a pretty public high school breakup.

Teenagers are cruel.

I felt a small pang of nostalgia, wishing he was here to see the house in person. I could hear him rolling through all the insults he'd sling about every small imperfection. Sam's coping mechanism was well-armed insults. It's his most endearing quality—it might be his only endearing quality. Most times, he's a real nightmare.

My phone buzzed again, this time a video call from Ivy.

"Hey, world traveler," I greeted her as her face filled the screen. Ivy's hair was pulled tightly into a bun, and a stack of books loomed in the background.

"Wren!" Ivy's voice was warm, like a harmonious hug for your soul.

"Tell me it's not worse than the photos. Did you get catfished?"

I turned the camera around and gave her a view of the living room. "It's... cozy."

Ivy laughed. "Cozy is another word for haunted. Has anything moved by itself?"

"Fortunately, there's nothing here to move yet."

I smiled, though I couldn't help but glance at the shadows pooling in the far corners of the room. A strange play on light that felt a little *unnatural*. I'd never say it out loud for fear of making it a reality, but there was something eerie about this house.

"So..." Ivy paused, "What's the plan? Painting or exorcism?"

"Actually..." I said, "I found a flyer for an art auction downtown tonight." I reached into my bag and pulled out the crumpled flyer. "I thought I'd check it out and find something unique and *new.*"

"One day in the suburbs, and you're already shopping the yard sales," Ivy teased.

"It's an auction, Ivy—it's probably dead people's art," I said as I tossed my keys onto the granite island.

"Just don't spend your entire life savings on something weird."

"Noted," I said, rolling my eyes. "I have to unpack the car; Call you later."

As soon as the call disconnected, the silence crashed into me like a ton of bricks. The natural sounds of the house hadn't quite acclimated to my ears. Every small creak and click was a false alarm that made my eyes dart. But it was the damp, nearly deafening silence that chilled me. I shook my head and told myself that the lack of furniture made the echoes worse.

Once I moved in, it would feel like *home*.

Home.

Another unnerving thought that I wasn't ready to think about. I'd run away from my apartment and left everything behind. My family, my job, my clients, any friends I had except Sam and Ivy— who would have tracked me down in the Sahara if that's where I'd gone. They were inescapable, and I was grateful for their commitment.

I'd have to learn to think of a different place, *this place*, when I thought of the word home. Not the dive bar I lived near that I'd made my regular place to relax. Not the Mexican place I ordered from every Thursday, as if I were an addict getting their fix—only my addiction was birria burritos and cheese pupusas.

Surprisingly, I wasn't even a little afraid—apprehensive, certainly. But afraid? Absolutely not.

What scared me was staying stuck in a relationship that had nearly killed me. What frightened me to my core was waking up ten years from now and realizing that nothing had changed, and I was still living a life filled with hollow promises to myself. That was scarier than any ghost, haunted house, or weird new town.

I put my hand on the banister, and with a deep breath, I dared to adventure upstairs. There were two bedrooms—a primary suite with an attached full bathroom and an expansive second bedroom for my gallery and editing office. It was why I bought this house. Both rooms were incredible. My entire apartment could have fit inside just one of these rooms, but it really was the natural light and the architecture that pulled me in and swallowed me whole.

The photos of the listing looked like art, and I didn't have to be *sold* into spending my entire life savings on this place. I willingly did it.

I slowly pushed open the door to the primary bedroom, easily the largest room in the house. My eyes were immediately drawn to the brightness that washed over the grand fireplace. It stood stoically next to the magnificent floor-to-ceiling arched windows,

As I approached, I ran my fingers over the details, instantly recognizing how intricate the craftsmanship was on the masonry and the care taken around the hand-carved mantel, worn smooth in some places from years of use.

They didn't make houses like this anymore. The return on investment was lost somewhere between affordability and demand.

The room smelled faintly of woodsmoke and something... unruly. The smell of lives lived layered over top of the stagnant must of vacancy. If *history* had a distinct smell, it would be the scent swirling in the open air of this room.

The light rushed in, free to scatter itself on the polished plank floors—unobstructed by curtains or blinds.

This room was beautiful...

This was home, and I could feel it welcoming me.

✳✳✳

I found the auction house just as the sun had set. It was tucked cautiously away in a narrow side street, the kind of place you wouldn't notice unless you were looking for it. I didn't know if that was strategy or poor marketing, but there were far more people here than I'd imagined—it was almost a full house.

The interior smelled like polished wood and dust. Rows of folding chairs lined the front of a small stage. I sat in the back, scanning the catalog I'd been handed at the door. An older gentleman politely asked to sit next to me.

Realizing I was taking up two seats, I quickly moved my bag, apologized, and kindly offered him the vacant space.

He had a friendly face, and years of wisdom were evident in the creases on the outer edge of his eyes. He settled in and introduced himself.

"Charlie Whittaker." He smiled and reached his hand over to shake mine.

"Wren Rivers." Meeting his eyes with a smile.

"First time?" He questioned me with a deep curiosity glittering in his eye.

"I'm sorry?" I replied, unsure of what he meant.

"At the auction?"

"Oh—Yes—Just moved here today." I wondered if it was because I looked out of place or if he was just a regular. "I'm in the old Estate neighborhood, the backside of the farm," I added.

"You must have friends in high places. Those homes are highly sought after." His eyes were now wide with wonder.

"Couldn't be... I practically stole it from the previous owner," I nodded as the auctioneer prepared himself on stage. Most of the art being auctioned this evening were landscapes and portraits of people whose identities had been lost in the hustle and bustle of life *moving on.*

I thumbed through slowly. The portrait of a woman who'd pretended to be a man and infiltrated the United States Army to train as a medic. A portrait of a man who forged paths on the Underground Railroad.

The delicate paintings of scenes and landscapes of places that no longer existed—now replaced with convenience stores and condominiums.

On the last page, it hit me.

Lot #42: Untitled, 1600s (Estimated)

The oil painting was dark, even strange. It was a blurred figure staring longingly out a window. Although it was described as another portrait, it felt like something so much more. The man's frayed edges seemed unfinished, his features shifting under the gloss of the pages the longer I stared at them.

His expression was one of mourning. He looked twisted and tortured, maybe even broken—standing and waiting for something that would never arrive. The rawness of his expression made my heart ache with melancholy. I couldn't explain the connection or why a *painting* made me feel so emotional.

But this could be what art was. It's made to make you feel something profound. Anything I had ever hung on my walls up to this point couldn't have been art because I'd never had such a response.

My photographs were good. I'd made a career selling them at shows and events not unlike this auction. They were in magazines, galleries, and private commissions from celebrities I can't name. But they were not art the way that these paintings were art.

There was a discernable difference between a photo I'd snapped in just a second and a painting that took years of layering to complete. A painting such as this was a labor of love, especially so long ago without technological advancements.

The auctioneer's voice called for bids on earlier lots, but I barely heard him. The speed of his bid-taking blurred together his intentions, and my thoughts overpowered him, focused steadily on Lot #42.

My God. If just a photo of the timeless piece of art had made my pulse race with excitement, how would I feel when faced with the actual painting?

"Lot forty-two," the auctioneer announced at last, gesturing to the painting, which leaned delicately on a large easel. Far larger than I'd expected, darker than I'd ever imagined. I tried not to stare too deeply, fearing it would trap me in a trance, but I locked eyes with it and felt it grab me.

I was caught, like quicksand, from childhood movies. My vision fixed on the man like I was daydreaming, but I was completely aware that I couldn't move.

But truthfully, I didn't *want* to stop staring. Every glitter, every shadow, every sparkle pulled me in further. I could hear the faint tenor of a voice. We were having a casual conversation about the weather and the carriage ride he'd taken that morning to fetch some obscure item from the market.

I am not a believer in love at first sight. I think it's unbelievable. Fiction, made up by novelists and screenwriters.

But, whatever I felt now... seemed a lot like what someone experiencing the phenomenon might feel—except the man I was falling for... wasn't even real.

He was in a painting.

I didn't need anyone to tell me that *this* was crazy. It sounded wild. As the announcer read the details and the bidding processes were prepared, it was mentioned that the sale of this piece had failed previously.

"Shame... It's quite a lovely painting," Charlie mumbled beside me, and I jumped at his words. I'd forgotten he was even there. I nodded nervously, hoping he hadn't realized he'd startled me.

"Bidding starts at one hundred dollars."

Silence. The room's din dropped to a deafening emptiness. Each piece prior had a chatter that followed its announcement. Some wanted to bid, some considered bidding, others wished they could bid—and they discussed it, leading to conversation that hummed delicately in the room, filling it with excitement and the thrill of the bidding battle. But this one?

Silence.

My hand shot up before I could think twice. A force compelling it upward despite the fact that I'd tried to set it down or stop it from rising. My hand remained in the air against my will.

Charlie smiled at me. "That's a nice portrait, Wren." He paused. "He'll be a lovely addition to your new home." His voice felt distant, almost paranormal, as he whispered his congratulations— *before I'd even won it.*

"One hundred dollars," the auctioneer said. "Do I hear one-fifty?"

No one else moved. The room seemed lifeless, as if the once very alive bidders were all now just mannequins... sitting in chairs, holding space but not real. Their expressions were unmoved, and no one acknowledged this beautiful piece of art's existence while it was on stage.

I wondered how that could be when it screamed for attention. The paint practically crawled off the canvas and danced with my sadness in the room, beckoning me to *feel* it.

How could I be the only one it called to?

"Sold!" the auctioneer said with a snap of his gavel. "To the lady in the back."

I blinked, realizing what had just happened. I bought it. It was *mine.* My heart pounded in my chest as a wave of satisfaction settled over me. The painting was mine.

And I felt it had been waiting for me all along.

I looked to my left to talk to Charlie about it, but he was gone.

♫ "I Found" – Amber Run

CHAPTER 2

Home

He arrived a week later.

I'd already decided the piece would hang as the focal point in the overly bright living room. I'd obsessed over the placement, wanting the portrait to be brought back to life by being the center of attention. It was an ancient art long forgotten, so much so that it had no name, no signature—no creator.

I wanted it to be remembered, to be *thought* of.

My furniture from my apartment had finally arrived, and I realized rather quickly that the life I'd previously lived as 'Wren from the City' was a different Wren than the one I was actively becoming in the suburbs. The eclectic statues and high-gloss design of practically everything I owned looked out of place here.

It even felt like someone else had picked it out.

Maybe… all that I'd been through had finally started to change me. I wish I could say that it was me coming into myself, but this change was darker. I'd become more cynical and less trusting. My heart had been broken and betrayed one too many times, and this was a retreat, a grand *hermiting*.

The irony wasn't lost on me—how out of place I, too, must look standing delicately in the center of this old house in the middle of nowhere.

My behaviors were still all flash and fancy—I liked my gratification instant, and my patience was always *big-city* thin. My coffee order was still complicated and pretentious.

You can't convince me that macadamia nut milk tastes anything like oat milk. It doesn't, and I'll die on this hill.

Finding a way to slow down to a small-town pace would take practice. But I was glad to stop pretending that being overscheduled, understaffed, and always busy was a status symbol.

I'd felt like I was running out of air for too long. This steady incline I'd been relentlessly running up tore me into parts and pieces, and I left them all lying on the dead grass of someone else's front yard.

I'd recognized the disconnect midway through emptying my haphazardly packed boxes and hesitated. Holding a ceramic sphynx cat in one hand and a black glossy box that didn't open in the other. At a crossroads, I left the remnants of my former life untouched, shoving the boxes into what was meant to be my editing studio.

A little out of sight, out of mind, never hurt anyone.

It was clear that I wasn't ready to return to work, *not yet*. When art was your career, you had to be in the right mind for it. Without your mind connected fully to your heart, your product would be disconnected, unattached.

It wouldn't have the magic that made it what it was.

A loud knock at the heavy oak door revealed an impatient delivery person. Upon the loud opening of the door, a large lumber-framed package greeted me. The man handed me a clipboard to sign without so much as asking my name. We both glanced at the lumber box. He raised a brow as I scratched a shapeless scribble across the paperwork.

"Old art, huh?"

I nodded. "Yeah, something like that."

"It's... heavy." He shifted uncomfortably before returning to his truck. "Good luck." He called out as the sliding door slammed.

I chuckled, watching him drive off. His reaction had seemed strange... as if he was nervous or even afraid of the wooden box's contents. But I let it go. The folks here weren't the same as they were in the city. I was growing used to the weirdness of it all, which required me to look past a lot of odd behavior.

For a second, Charlie flashed across my mind. Our interaction was the oddest of them all. *Where had he gone?* I shook my head at the thought.

I studied the giant lumber frame carefully before grabbing the edge and attempting to lift it. I was met with a force that made it feel like the box had been super glued to the ground, and I let out a painful grunt.

There was absolutely no reason for this box to weigh this much. The painting wasn't that large, and most of these frames were delicately packed with soft materials to comfort and protect the art from damage. They certainly did not fill framed boxes with bricks or cement.

I'd packaged enough art in my life.

After an hour of using various tools and my legs with my back pressed against the walls for leverage, the lumber frame was finally home... in the center of the nearly empty living room.

I was tickled with excitement as I stared adoringly at the first piece of my new life. This wasn't just a painting to me—*no.*

It was a symbol of my fresh start.

After using every fiber of my being to get the painting inside, I felt like I had run a mile *and* been hit by a bus. My body ached in muscles I didn't know I had: thighs and *second* thighs.

I cracked the lumber frame lid open with a prybar, and a plume of dust billowed out from the top like a magic cloud. My delight at finally being reunited with the portrait was uncalled for.

A single white sheet of paper stared up at me, several layers of tape securing it to the outer frame as if they feared it would blow off.

"NO RETURNS."

It made me giggle. How many people were attempting to return art they bought at an auction? Signs were usually added after someone broke a rule or a reason made them necessary. Lessons learned are often solved with a sign.

I dusted the canvas with a cotton cloth, brushing off the bits of debris that had mysteriously gravitated toward the mystery man's delicate features. I admired his shape again, his face, and the dullness of his eyes, which seemed to yearn for life. Something tragic about how he stared out that window, waiting for something to happen—for an eternity.

"Welcome home," I whispered as I lifted the large, ornate frame. Chips and cracks I hadn't seen before littered the outer edge, evidence that this piece had not only seen a long life but a rough one, too. The painting was *light.* Peculiar for how heavy the box was—but I forced myself to create a logical explanation and prepped the painting for installation.

I'd hung a thousand art pieces in my life, mostly my own photographs. So, preparing this piece was second nature, with all of my tools laid out. I delicately placed the hangers into the wall studs and took great care in reinforcing the hanging wire on the rear of the piece.

I lifted it into place and carefully set it down on the hanger. Nearly out of breath from the entire exchange, I slowly stepped back and allowed myself a moment to admire the room. This painting was a part of me, now, a part of my life, and it looked like it belonged here.

The paint, as old as it was estimated to be, was in miraculously perfect condition—a miracle. Paint of this age had been known to disintegrate, dust away, and crumble with the harsh reality of time. This paint looked like it had just dried yesterday. Maybe it had gone through a restoration before being auctioned.

That was definitely it. *Restoration.*

I reached out and brushed my fingers gently against the ancient paint, over the slight ripples in the man's cheeks and across the smooth, velvety texture of his lips. My breath hitched slightly when a flash of a vision pierced my mind. The man, in the darkness, *alone.*

***

Hours later, I found myself feeling accomplished and genuinely satisfied after a hard day's work and enjoyed a very late dinner. If running on fumes were an Olympic sport, I'd have medals. The day had defeated me, and I was hanging onto my sanity by a mere thread.

I'd misplaced my phone twice and lost a hammer and two sets of screwdrivers—as if they had disappeared into thin air. I'd nearly fallen down the stairs *twice*, and my shirt was torn on a loose trim nail sticking out in the hall. My favorite shirt.

If I believed in such circumstances, I'd think that this *house* was trying to kill me. I scoffed at the absurdity just as the bulb in the dining room lamp let out a concerning hiss and left me in complete and utter darkness. A sigh released from my chest almost instinctively. Even my subconscious found the oddities of this house *normal.*

Perhaps murder was a bit harsh, but the house was definitely testing what little of my patience remained. My situation was unsurprising. This was my luck, so I sat in the dark, letting the shallow creeks and taps pulverize any courage I might have had. I lingered a little longer than I should have but took the darkness as a sign that perhaps it was time to retire, rest, and resume my efforts *tomorrow.*

I felt my way upstairs to my bedroom, guided by the soft glow of the lamp I'd left on for myself, still not acquainted with the floor plan enough to navigate it in the dark. And perhaps I was still afraid of what might lurk in the corners of these rooms I didn't know.

The eerie silence that had captivated me on my first night here had returned, but I was too exhausted to allow it to haunt me. I'd barely had the energy to turn off the bedside lamp. My eyes darted briefly across the room, looking for an apparition, a specter or a phantom, the cause of the day's mischief, but I saw nothing but empty shadows.

While tucked into the warmth of my bedding, I'd made never-ending lists of all that needed to be done. I needed *internet* and to buy a new sofa. I needed new lamps from this century and lightbulbs—LEDs, something with a bit more *stamina.*

And, I guess, a new toolbox to replace all I'd lost in the chaos of a new house. I knew I'd find the rogue tools immediately after purchasing new ones, but I was exhausted at the idea of continuing the search. It was time to call it off and invest in replacements.

That's just how my luck was turning over these days.

I sighed deeply at seeing the exponentially growing to-do list, letting its overwhelming vastness concern me. My anxiety vibrated in my head like a fly trapped. I still needed to organize my editing office and studio room so I could consider returning to work. I had to start paying off all the debt incurred during this move.

I wasn't ready to admit that I needed, more than anything, to get my life back to a place where I didn't feel like I was gasping for breath at the top of a lake that was trying to pull me down.

The overwhelming loneliness of a new life came with its own set of problems that I hadn't considered, but at least one perk was that no one was here to watch me fumble and fall over and over again. No one was here to witness the disaster I'd become.

My mistakes were secrets I could keep between my mind and my heart, and the privacy allowed me to make them freely. I didn't need the constant reminders of my failures looming over me in the tone of a disappointed mother. Or, in the painful eyes of a protective father who wished I was closer—wished I'd tried harder to make things work.

With my career.

With a man.

I sighed deeply, pulled the covers over my head, and relaxed into a deep sleep with images of a face too familiar seared into the darkness of my eyelids. The face from my portrait, the face of a man whose history eluded me.

I wanted his name and to hear his voice.

I wanted to know who had painted him in such a light and why they left his heart so unfinished. What story might he tell me?

A moment before I fully descended, I heard a floorboard groan in the distance. I told myself it was nothing, but deep down...

I knew better. Despite my overwhelming exhaustion, I didn't sleep well. I'd never been scared of the dark before, but that fear was becoming too certain of a reality. Or was I just scared of being alone?

***

It wasn't the peeking sunlight that pierced through the unprotected windows, still without blinds or curtains, that abruptly woke me. It was the icy chill that had consumed the room. As if it were no surprise, the furnace had stopped working during the night, and it wasn't until I emerged from the warmth I'd nested in through the night that I realized something was wrong.

I grabbed a robe and two sweaters and layered myself with heavy winter clothes as I adventured into the very old, very unfinished basement to diagnose the problem myself, especially if the problem required me to battle a yeti or build a snowman.

After three emergency calls to repair companies and two video calls with my handyman of a father, we determined that the pilot light had gone out. That was it.

Easy fix.

For someone else.

This was just another minor annoyance that I'd hoped was a mere coincidence and not the efforts of ghosts trying to shoo me from the home I now owned.

But... I didn't believe in ghosts, did I?

The technician who arrived to repair the furnace, buried deep in the basement, shifted uneasily as he saw the vast painting positioned directly in the living room. They stared at each other for a few moments before the kind man nodded to me and disappeared.

He was definitely the type who believed in ghosts.

He fled so quickly after repairing the furnace that he didn't even leave an invoice, and my wallet lived to fight another day.

Despite the delay and chaos of the morning, I was focused solely on unpacking the kitchen and planned on methodically organizing plates and utensils. Still, I kept drifting toward the living room—toward the painting of my mystery roommate, who wasn't much help with kitchen unpacking.

With no one to talk to, I had casual chats with him. Deciding how we'd split the chores and ultimately agreeing that it was only fair that I do the dishes, so long as he continues to stare meaninglessly out the window.

By early afternoon, I'd begged the universe for a distraction from unpacking, and when it didn't deliver, I grabbed my phone and called Sam. Sometimes, we must make our own fate. A greedy thought I didn't push away.

"Tell me everything's fine," I said the second he answered.

'Uh-oh," Sam replied, his voice layered with humorous concern. "What did the house do now?"

"Well... It scared the HVAC technician away." I paused, "Get this," I built unnecessary suspense, "The furnace pilot light went out last night. The house was so cold that I could see my breath when I woke up," my story recanted with an air of disbelief.

"Pilot lights go out, Wren," Sam said, annoyed. "But the technician—maybe he just saw your face and was terrified?"

I scoffed. "Just when I thought you were being helpful." I smiled, though Sam couldn't see my affectionate grin

"Are you sure you're not just a little lonely, like you're in a new place, town, clients, and everything is new? Maybe this is all a part of the process." Sam's teasing had gone, and he was being genuine.

"Probably—thank you," I murmured, hating to admit that he'd made me feel better and that he might be right.

God, I'd never tell him that. Ever.

"Give yourself a break, booboo. You're doing fine." His reassurance meant far more than he could know.

"Okay, I'll call you later. I need a nap."

***

I'd almost finished unpacking the kitchen, dining room, and bathrooms with minor injury or mischief. As I finalized putting the decorative touches in the luxurious en suite bathroom, I decided if it was well within my rights to soak my body in hot water.

And determined that, without question, *it was.*

The muscle aches that terrorized me were relentless. I could barely lift my legs to climb the stairs. Taking one step at a time, I managed to arrive at the base of a tub made for a queen.

I watched the old claw-foot tub slowly fill, the steam rising like an inviting hot soup for my soul. I dropped my robe, feeling the air hit my body with a chill.

Perhaps it was the vulnerability of being naked in my home, alone, but I instantly felt as if I was being watched. I felt a deep, knowing stare observing me—glaring intently at my naked body.

I know it sounds crazy, but it felt like whatever was watching me could see more than my skin. It was as if they were staring into the ugliest parts of my broken soul. The parts I wanted someone to see far less than my bare breasts.

I felt a surge of embarrassment rise to my cheeks, flushing them against the cold air of the tile bathroom.

I quickly pulled the shower curtain to one side, blocking the window, and a bit of relief washed over me as I stepped into the frothy, soapy water. I lowered myself in, and the hot water met the resistance of my tightened muscles with a massaging warmth.

I let out the deepest sigh as the tingling numbness of the hot water eased out the pain that had settled in the crevices, searing me with a comfort that felt both painful and satisfying.

I tipped my head onto the high back of the tub and let the water engulf me, closing my eyes for what felt like only a few moments. When I opened them, the water was lukewarm and had started to cool into an uncomfortable embrace.

Against the angry pull of gravity, I lifted myself up, bracing my hands on each side of the tub, my body heavy as the ground fiercely attempted to pull me down onto it.

One pair of mismatched pajamas, the only silk pillowcase I could find, and a big glass of ice-cold water later, I crawled into bed. Covering myself with a den of blankets just like I had the night before. Attempting to bury myself in the most comfortable of cotton graves, my arms tragically struggling to lift the layers of blankets over my head. I admired my small cavern of blankets, knowing that it protected me from the unsettling noises of my old, ancient, *haunted* house. The thick layers dulling the noises that sought to rattle me and keep me from another night of sleep.

As I drifted off, a soft whisper brushed past my ear.

"Goodnight, Little Bird."

A deep, handsome whisper sent a seductive chill down my spine and into my core. I let it tickle me for a few minutes. I let it linger in the hollows of my ears as if it were a kiss from a passionate lover. A love song written to the beats of my violently afraid heart.

But as soon as I'd realized, half-asleep, that I was very much alone in this bed and this room.

In this house—my eyes snapped open, and I manically flipped the blankets down and slowly scanned the vast, empty room.

It was empty. Not even the subtle stir of a distant shadow through the magnificent windows. *Nothing.*

Only the echo of that phantom whisper hung in the air, twirling around the room like smoke from a blown-out candle. I snatched my phone quickly from the nightstand and struggled to calm my fingers enough to unlock it.

Sam was a night owl. He'd be awake, so I tapped out a message with my still-shaking fingers.

> **Me:** OK. It's haunted for real.
>
> **Sam:** O_o
>
> **Sam:** You bought a Victorian murder house?
>
> **Sam:** Side note: THIS is why it was a good deal.
>
> **Sam:** This was identified as a possible outcome early on.
>
> **Sam:** AKA I told you so bitch
>
> **Me:** No? idk. They have to disclose that.
>
> **Me:** I heard something. A whisper. A man's voice.
>
> **Sam:** Omg Wren.
>
> **Me:** …
>
> **Sam:** Be the thing ghosts are afraid of.
>
> **Me:** LMAO what??
>
> **Sam:** No seriously. Show no fear. Be scarier than the ghost.
>
> **Sam:** You have the face for it.
>
> **Me:** Blocked. Reported. UNSUBSCRIBE.
>
> **Sam:** Just saying. You should at least sage the place.
>
> **Sam:** Or perform an exorcism. Do you own a crucifix?
>
> **Me:** No. Do you?
>
> **Sam:** I'm gay, Wren, not a vampire slayer.

I snorted, tension breaking just a little. But my eyes still flicked to the empty shadows in the room. The whisper had been real. Hadn't it? I don't remember when I'd fallen asleep, but I'd certainly tried not to.

♫ "Creep" – Radiohead

CHAPTER 3

Bold

A loud clatter from the kitchen.

My heart leaped into my throat, and my adrenaline rushed me, sending me into fight or flight. This house was keeping me on my toes.

This time, I chose *fight*.

Sam's encouragement echoed in my head: "Show no fear."

I rushed downstairs with a broom in my hand.

Nothing.

The house was silent again, but my pulse pounding kept me on edge. Shadows from branches outside the kitchen window spattered across the light tile floor, but no other movement was detected. The air was completely still.

The doors remained locked and closed. Every piece of misplaced junk and trash was precisely where I had left it the night before. I knew because it haunted me in a way that this house hadn't. I spent at least fifteen minutes in the bath, remembering and forgetting that I had left this room in disarray.

"Hello?" My voice felt small, insignificant in the emptiness of the house.

No response.

I scanned the kitchen and noticed something odd—a stack of plates I hadn't yet found a place for had been moved and positioned somewhere I hadn't put them.

I didn't leave them there. I know that I hadn't...

Had I?

"Right," I muttered, "Plates just move on their own." I walked over to them, relaxing the broom down to my side as I placed my hand delicately on the stack. They felt warm with a current running through them, and they snapped electricity at my fingers. I pulled my hand away quickly.

What the hell was that?

I could now hear Sam's voice screaming in my head: *Run, don't investigate.* Instead, I set down my broom, grabbed the charged plates, and restacked them.

Where they belonged.

My nerves were now tingling with every movement. The house didn't feel dangerous. It just felt alive, watching, waiting. After all, reorganizing plates was a far cry from murder. Perhaps the ghosts that were haunting were just particular about dish placement.

I walked back toward the bedroom, my aches from yesterday not *entirely* gone. I had very much been looking forward to a day of rotting in bed while reading something smutty on my Kindle.

The painting.

It wasn't the same. The figure, the face I'd come to know so well, had shifted ever so slightly—his blurred features and unfinished edges now more distinct, his head turned outward, just a fraction, as though he were now staring straight at me.

Staring into my heart, asking me to give it up.

A chill ran down my spine. I blinked and shook my head, convincing myself it was my imagination. Sleep deprivation, too much caffeine, ibuprofen overdose. That's all. New house creeps, an overactive imagination, and loneliness—the thing I didn't want to admit.

I stared for a moment longer and was startled by the loud rattle of my phone vibrating on the kitchen counter.

Ivy.

"Wren!" Her excitement whenever I answered her video calls never got old. She'd been in Japan for over a year and was on a completely different schedule than me. Despite the insane time difference, she always made sure she calculated and called me at reasonable times.

"How's it going?" Her excitement and cheer starkly contrasted the building tension in my *maybe* haunted house.

"Uh, fine," I said, letting out a deep sigh as the anxiety and adrenaline faded from my chest, loosening me slightly. I tilted my head back and forth to let my neck stretch in between.

"This house is... a lot," I added, running my fingers through my hair, the concern obvious in my expression.

"Define a lot," Ivy said, her tone turning curious.

I hesitated, knowing the walls were listening. "The house is weird. It's playing pranks on me," I said, sighing.

"And I am convinced my painting... *moved.*" My eyes widened. "Like the painting looks like a different painting entirely."

"I swear I told you *not* to buy anything weird, girl." Ivy swooned at the idea. "But, do tell me more."

"It's probably nothing," I said quickly. I got it at the auction I told you about. It's just an old piece of art with no known history, really." I smiled.

"It's just been a long couple of days."

"Send me a picture," she said, "I'll look into it."

I snapped a quick photo and sent it over while we continued catching up.

"Oh, that definitely has a vibe. It *is* beautiful. I'll do some digging and see if I come up with anything."

"You're the best," I smiled as I fiddled with my new coffee maker.

Falling back to sleep felt like an improbability. Therefore, coffee was a now a requirement.

"Call me later, love you."

I eyed the painting long after Ivy had disappeared. Finally, I decided to take it off the wall, dragging it with strength I'd just discovered all the way up the stairs and mounting it above the grand fireplace in my bedroom.

As soon as I stepped back and stared deeply into the man's eyes, I knew *this* was where he was supposed to be. Not downstairs, in a room that was barely lived in, but here in this room. With me. So that I could keep my eye on him and ensure it wasn't *him* causing all of the chaos in my house.

✳✳✳

I lay back on the bed, exhaling slowly, my eyes fixed on the ceiling as I tried to quiet the rattling of thoughts. It had been a long, strange couple of days, and I needed something to distract me, clear my head, and ground myself back in my body. I needed to feel something other than suspicion and calamity.

I closed my eyes, letting my fingers drift across my skin, focusing on the soft hum of sensation that began to build just under the surface. My breath grew shallow as I surrendered to the familiar rhythm, exactly what I knew would take me over the edge.

I pulled my hands away. I lifted them above my head, an inherent knowing that I was no longer in control of the rush of warmth that brushed over my body

My body tingled under the movement as the touch grazed gently over the places that made me vibrate with uncontrollable pleasure. I'd felt the tension in the room but brushed it aside. I lost myself in the touch, which gave me *exactly* what I craved.

My heart raced, picking up the pace, and my breath rolled from my mouth in uneven pants that coincided with the downward strokes. Just a little longer, as I held back the rising pressure building. I slowly formed a subtle arch in my back to catch the right angle of the slight caress pressed against me.

Without warning, I lightly whimpered as I tightened around it and came plummeting from the release.

My eyes snapped open when I realized where my hands were. Far above my head, not anywhere near...

Had I imagined the entire thing? Did I dream an orgasm?

Had it been so long that I was daydreaming incredibly realistic—

A cold breeze ghosted across bits of my bare skin, and the burst wasn't just cool—it was frosted like an ice-cold breeze blown purposefully across my exposed body. I winced at the rushing, frigid air as it littered my skin with unstoppable chills.

My gaze darted quickly to the window, but it was shut tight. Where were breezes and gusts of cold air coming from? I understood the house was drafty, but at some point, these drafts were uncharacteristically powerful.

My heart was hammering in my chest, blurring out all other noise, and my vision fixated around me in a fear I'd never known.

I pulled my robe on and twisted the tie tightly when I noticed the blanket I'd laid delicately over me had fallen to the floor. I hadn't kicked it off or cast it aside, *no. I had not.*

I slowly scanned the room, every shadow suddenly leaping out at me with a life I hadn't imagined. Someone was playing tricks on me, and I needed to get to the bottom of it. I was tired of feeling like a guest in a house that was mine, honestly... I was just plain *tired.*

"Okay. Very funny. You've made your point." My voice was unsteady with fear.

My heart was confused and cluttered—going from a perfectly timed orgasm to a vomit-inducing fear was a wild ride I hadn't prepared for.

Vomit.

A sickness seared through me. I felt it, but I took a deep breath and choked it back down, my hands clasped tightly over my mouth. I ran for the bathroom. My body didn't take kindly to being taken advantage of by ghosts, revenants, specters... *anyone.*

And it let out everything I'd tried to hold in, emptying every last bit of warmth I had left in me.

Disgusting.

I thought as I took a few deep breaths and leaned my body against the cold tile of the bathroom floor, letting it fight away the heat of my fear and illness, but the sour heat crawled back up my throat, and my stomach lurched again, draining me of any energy or fight I had in me.

A soft, intimate chuckle echoed through the room, but I felt the heat of this laugh against my cheek. It was warm. As if whoever had unleashed it was amused and undeniably male—the same voice that had whispered to me last night.

The recognition of it sent my heart into overdrive, and I slowly crawled out of the bathroom, twisting my body to look in every corner for the *who*.

Every nerve was on alert when my eyes suddenly locked on the painting above the mantle, where the figure seemed sharper than before. His head tilted slightly, his blurred face completely focused, and his grin pulled to one side.

As if he'd been *watching* me.

"Oh my god," I whispered, my heart slamming against the inside of my chest. It felt like hammers inside of me trying to bludgeon their way out.

It was *him*.

The rational part of my brain screamed that this wasn't real— that I was tired, that my imagination was running wild.

But the fact that I could still feel him—here—in this room with me. His presence lingered, wrapping around me like a snake, coiling me into paralysis. This proved to me that any justification was doing myself a disservice. I was being fucked with, toyed with, and there *was* a ghost in that painting.

He *had* intruded on my private moment *in my room*... Anger started to replace the empty parts that sickness created. My stomach was cramped with fury, and a heat rose to my cheeks.

"Who... *are* you?" I demanded, my voice stronger.

It was the question I'd wanted to ask since the moment I'd seen the painting in that catalog. But why *the hell* was he putting his creepy ghost hands on my body?

"Now, now, Little Bird, we mustn't ruin the moment."

I froze, and every hair on my body stood up. I was holding my breath... I knew it because my vision was blurring. I was going to pass out if I didn't—*breathe.*

I forced myself to take a deep breath in as I nearly collapsed onto the floor. I grabbed the edge of my bed and pulled myself up into it. I snatched my phone clumsily, knocking over a framed picture of Sam, Ivy, and me. The glass shattered and fell to the floor with a chaotic clang of high-pitched tings.

I tapped a message to Ivy, relying heavily on autocorrect. The anger still trapped in my body made my hands tremble, unable to tap against the letter that I needed.

I felt a rise in my throat when another wave of sickness threatened to send me back to the bathroom, but I fought back, swallowing it down as I pressed send.

Me: Painting talks.
Me: Call me. Help.

My eyes drifted back to the painting again. I wiped my face with my arm, dripping with the sweat of my fury, and I stared deeply into the painting, prepared not to blink for even a moment until I confirmed it *wasn't* alive.

♫ "Trouble" – Valerie Broussard

CHAPTER 4

Boundaries

I'd had my fair share of one-night stands and hookups. I was an artist who lived in a big city full of choices.

Every instance of *temporary fondness* felt like placeholders, but none were as degrading as having a *ghost* intrude on your personal endeavors. That phantom touch, the way my body betrayed its good sense under his influence, even the sound of that taunting and yet painfully delicious voice. It replayed in my head like a bad dream I couldn't *un*-have.

I dragged myself out of bed, my bare feet padding against the hardwood, and made my way to the enormous bathroom.

A hot shower. *That's what I needed.*

It would clear my mind, help me start the day, and ease the aches that made it feel like I had run a marathon in my sleep.

Exhaustion from the hauntings was ruining my life, and my body was feeling it too.

At least here, I could scrub off how *dirty* I felt.

The water cascaded over me, and my muscles loosened. It refused to settle despite filling my head with the roar of the water over my ears. Every time I closed my eyes, I saw the blurred figure from the painting, his head tilted slightly and his smug grin.

And worse, a jolt of pleasure reverberated through my body as I felt the touch again. The velvet pressure between my legs almost dropped me, but it wasn't *him*. Only the realistic memory of what had happened.

I wrapped myself in a towel and stood before the bathroom mirror, wiping the steam that had settled as moisture from the searing hot temperature. My reflection was barely recognizable, my cheeks hollowing, and dark circles deepened around my eyes.

"No more," I muttered. "Whoever—whatever you are—you're leaving. *Today.*"

A promise that I intended to keep.

✷✷✷

I had reluctantly spent a few hours researching ways to eliminate unwanted spirits. Google was less than helpful, offering little practical advice and more absurd suggestions. I found myself down a Reddit rabbit hole of sage bundles and salt lines before I finally snapped my laptop shut.

"This is stupid," I muttered, pacing the living room. "It's just a dumb piece of art." I paused.

"I'll get rid of it."

Just as I was prepared to engage, Ivy texted.

Ivy: I have painting leads. Everything ok?

Me: Things got... weird

Ivy: Details?

Me: I think the ghost participated in my self-pleasure.

Ivy: wtf

Ivy replied quickly.

And again.

Ivy: Two questions: 1. Did you like it? and 2. Are you on drugs?

Me: No drugs, I wish.

Me: Then it would be explainable.

Me: I think I should toss it. It was only $100.

Ivy: Wait. So, you liked it?

Me: Not answering that.

Ivy: I'll call later.

I couldn't help but smile. It felt like the first time I'd done that in weeks. My entire life felt like it was spiraling out of control, and I hadn't even returned to work yet, significantly behind schedule.

✳✳✳

I attempted to pull the art off the wall above the mantle for three hours, but it was stuck—*permanently affixed.* It had ghostly glued itself to the wall, making it impossible for me to dispose of it. I collapsed onto the floor, out of breath and completely exhausted.

It was fighting back.

While my body felt like it had fought off a grizzly bear, I still manically paced, thoughts thrumming through my mind about how one might *unstick* a haunted object that you purposefully placed in the most private room in your house. If I'd continued, I might have worn a path on the floor where my feet had stepped back and forth for hours. I was determined to reclaim my home at any cost.

I knew now that it was not merely haunted but that I'd invited in the devil, and I was tired of him intruding on my healing process.

I couldn't have a fresh start with a ghost from the 1600s musting up my living quarters. I couldn't live completely covered in clothing, afraid of what he might *see.* I couldn't explain moving objects or broken things if clients came to visit my gallery. Or ruined photos in the studio area.

And, *God forbid,* I meet someone and want to invite them here.

Imagine the horrifying look on a man's face when I asked if he was bothered by the possibility of ghostly *intrusions* by a magical man from the 1600s that haunted my bedroom.

It would certainly be inevitable, wouldn't it? I was not about to be in a *throuple* with a ghost. Absolutely not. The thought enraged me. I stood, squaring my shoulders, completely out of ideas *for now,* and bargaining was all I had left.

"Here's the deal. You're not welcome here. Whatever, whoever you are... you need to leave."

I stared deeply into the features of the face. The smirk he'd had last night was gone. Perhaps he'd lost it when I attempted to pry his frame off my wall.

Or maybe it was when I'd started swinging a bat at it, crumbling the old plaster walls on either side of him. The dust had scattered everywhere, and since he was still firmly secured, the attempt had only created more work for me when I had to clean up the broken plaster and dust.

I planted my hands firmly on my hips, and the only sound in the room was my hesitant breathing as I prepared for a *painting* to talk to me. The air shifted slightly, enough to make my skin pebble.

"Leave?" The voice was back, smooth and mocking, but he felt even closer this time, as if he'd coiled his arms around me and whispered delicately into my ear.

"Oh, Wren, but I'm having fun."

My breath caught in my throat. My eyes snapped to the painting, but the figure remained still, his face newly shrouded in darker shadow as if he were now hiding from me, being *coy*.

"I'm—I'm serious," I said, my voice trembling despite trying to declare my order as a demand.

"Get. Out."

Another chuckle, amused. "But why would I do that? You invited me in, didn't you? I *think—*"

"You don't think—you're a painting!" I interrupted him.

"Wren." He purred my name, tickling me in all the right places.

"I think you're enjoying my company far more than you're willing to admit."

Heat flushed my cheeks, the memory of last night flashing through my mind. I clenched my fists, pushing the embarrassment aside.

"I didn't invite you. You *intruded*. There's a difference."

"Oh, intruded, did I?" His voice was practically a song.

"It didn't seem like you minded too much when you came for me."

My pulse quickened, equal parts rage and something even more dangerous. "You're disgusting."

My voice was drenched in malice and disgust.

"If the truth is so vile, then perhaps I am." He was still mocking me.

"And I'm curious, tell me, Little Bird—why fight so hard? You could enjoy it, you know?" He paused as if he were reciting poetry.

"I could make it worth your while."

I stepped back, my heart pounding, my face heated with anger.

"Stay away from me. Stay out of my life."

"Is that really what you desire?" His tone was still velvet and smooth, gently wrapping around my entire being like a comfortable cloak.

"You could banish me. It's possible. I won't make it easy, and I'll 'intrude' as you say, in other areas. Or, you could let me stay." The voice paused. "I've long waited for a *Little Bird* like you."

I couldn't breathe. The floor was falling from under me, and I was tumbling down. I was torn between the primal pull of his words and the overwhelming urge to find a way—*any* way—to banish him for *good*.

"Get out," I whispered, my voice cracking in fear that I knew he could feel. It was palpable, tangible. My hands were ice cold, down to the bones, my heart racing as if it might burst from my chest and clatter down the hallway.

The lights flickered and then plunged the room into darkness. I'd never been afraid of the dark before, and now—I was considering sleeping with every light in the house on. I felt his breath along the nape of my neck and gently on my collarbone. He was *so close*. But the room was dark, blackened by the night, and I was helpless in my urge to repel him.

The light returned, filling the room instantly with a bright, inescapable golden glow. The voice was gone. The air settled, and the tension cleared as quickly as it had built. I thought the brief feeling of safety might pull some of the tension from my shoulders and neck, but I remained stiff.

I backed away from the painting slowly, my eyes locked on it.

"This isn't over," I said. "Ronan," a name slipped from my mouth, and I jumped back, my hands smacking over my lips as if I'd said something *evil*.

Ronan.

"There you are, Little Bird," He whispered as I felt him fully fade.

That was his name. I felt it flutter and reverberate back through my body when I said it. It felt comfortable—like I'd said it a thousand times before.

And I knew, now, Ronan was watching *everything* I did.

♫ "Hands To Myself" – Selena Gomez

CHAPTER 5

Control

It had been weeks since I'd told Ronan to leave.

He'd crawled back into his painting, and I hadn't seen even a whisper of evidence that he was present. That was until he started testing to see if his existence still angered me. His periodic presence motivated me to concoct a little plan of my own.

"I know you're there," I said, my voice steady despite the chill crawling up my spine, its tendrils feeling like the feet of hundreds of small spiders.

"You think I can't tell when you're thinking about me," I quipped.

Two could play his game of incessant seduction and malicious foreplay. He thought it was just *Ronan* who could make Wren weak, but the *Little Bird* had a few advantages.

I was alive.

And I wasn't an ancient ghost from a time long ago. I had modern solutions to *ancient* problems.

"I know when you're watching me. I can feel your eyes penetrate the walls when you play voyeur." I teased him.

I dropped my sweater off in the hall.

"I know when you're peeking out along the edges of that canvas, *praying* to whatever God you believe in, that I'll turn toward you." I pulled my shirt over my head and dropped it onto the floor. My chest on full display. "That you'll get just a glimpse."

I waited for the cool breeze that was inevitable when he was awake.

I slowly unbuttoned my jeans. "I can feel your breath when you see me unburdened by my clothes." I dropped them to the floor and stepped out of them.

"When you're pawing at the edges of the paint to *come* to me," I slid the last layer of lace down until it landed on the floor.

I climbed onto the bed, arching my back slightly, and crawled like a lioness into the den of blankets. Slowly laying myself down and pressing my hands down deep between my legs, thumbing my fingers over my entire body while I whispered out.

"Ronan," my hitched breath and low groans playfully exaggerated, enticing the specter to come for me.

I'd laid my trap. An exorcism required a manifestation, and with Ronan fully *in* the painting, I needed to lure him out. I needed to trap him in this reality to cleanse him from the house and from the art.

He'd once invaded my private event. I made a lofty assumption, naively, that he'd be unable to stop himself from doing it again.

I imagined a ghost trapped in a painting didn't get *much* satisfaction, but it felt like Ronan had.

But he took longer than I expected to respond. The heat of my body began rising faster than I'd thought by just *thinking* about him watching me. Just thinking about *him* at all caused my body to tremble and flinch.

Instead, my trap slowly turned too real as I realized that I was bringing myself closer and closer with each thought of him. Each whisper of his name that was meant as a façade turned its back on me and pressed into me deeper, making me squirm in an unrelenting passion.

My mouth quivered as the release building in me grew larger. I could feel the violence in it.

I could stop.

I could stop.

I would stop, just as he—

No. I couldn't stop.

Before I could change directions or even *think* about making a different decision, a fierce yelp filled my throat and landed delicately on my lips. I let the release rush over my entire body.

What had started as a manipulative plan to lure a ghost out for exorcism resulted in an ethereal moment of euphoric pleasure. I'd never done this to myself before, not at all like this.

A pulsating tightness in between my legs left me begging for the real thing, but I was elated that I hadn't stopped myself from writhing and twisting in the eruption I'd caused inside of my body.

I lay quietly in the stillness, unwilling to move a single muscle, all of them too heavy and relaxed to even consider picking up the mess of clothes I'd littered the floor with.

That was tomorrow's problem. And now, I needed a new plan.

✳✳✳

I'd spent the last four hours editing photographs I'd taken for a client last week. I twisted my neck and felt the tension pull back on me. I stood, stretching and pulling the tightness from an exhausted frame.

I hadn't worked in weeks, so I was grateful for the opportunity to disconnect from my haunted life. Also, the debt loomed over me like a shadow, a different kind of haunting but equally terrifying.

It was faint, barely there, but I'd felt Ronan's presence again. He'd been watching me work for hours. I couldn't tell if he was waiting for me to acknowledge him or just enthralled with modern technology.

"Why don't you show yourself?" I asked calmly, becoming too familiar with his presence. The silence I left when I didn't keep trying to entice him stretched on, and I felt an odd tingling in the room lingering through the air.

It wasn't a commitment but a consideration.

The shadows of the room began to twist, rippling against reality, moving in a way the light shouldn't. My breath caught in my throat as he stepped fully into my view. I don't know why, but I imagined that when I finally saw the ghastly visage, he would be a small framed shape, with a sheet overtop with eye holes cut in.

I didn't envision something my nightmares were made of—no, not at all. I slowly moved backward, reaching for the door handle behind me. I grabbed it, rattling it as I clumsily tried to open it without looking, without any coordination in my panic. It sprang free, and the door flung open behind me. I almost fell into the hall, losing my footing as the pressure I'd pushed the door with released.

I ran toward my bedroom. My body panicked, my hands trembling in an all-consuming fear. What had I been *thinking?* That my roommate was a friendly ghost? That I was dealing with an apparition that wanted to befriend me and play cards?

Phantoms don't haunt this world looking for friends. They haunt this world with evil intentions, with the intent to devour souls or brains. Or other body parts. Whatever the movies tell you ghosts do. They're never good. They're always evil.

And this one looked the part.

I glanced at the painting above the mantle, begging my mind to tell me it was simply making this up. My eyes squished shut—hard. Afraid to find out the truth. But I took a deep breath and opened them wide.

My vision cleared and settled on the painting, *praying* that it was there—intact, exactly as I'd bought it from the auction.

But the delicately painted, unfinished face and form had vanished entirely. The painting was just a smear of darkness, looking like the corner of an empty room with no purpose.

I turned quickly, panicking for an escape.

But I met a wall of darkness and shadow. He was no longer just a voice or an ominous presence but a tangible *being.* His eyes—dark and gleaming, locked onto mine, a mischievous glint playing in his irises.

"Hello, Little Bird," It sounded like a song—his voice smooth and delectable, like fine chocolate melting on your tongue.

"It seems you've *missed* me."

Perhaps this was a mental thing. I'd had a tough year—after Evan—maybe I'd snapped. Maybe I'd unlocked a whole new layer of crazy, even for me. But just thinking that man's name right before I died brought vomit to my mouth.

I was staring. I couldn't take my eyes off of him. He was frightening, but *my God*, he was also beautiful. I'd never considered how beautiful something so tragic might appear to be. If *this* was what I saw before I died, then I was good with it.

I could hear Ivy recant my departure on the stage of my funeral, "But, she will rest in peace because he was a *sexy* ghost," and I smiled. I closed my eyes again, taking as many deep breaths as possible. A tang of blood in the back of my throat from panting in fear tingled my tongue.

My pulse hammered in my ears, a sound I couldn't ignore, but I asked him anyway.

"What—the hell *are* you?" I begged him to answer. I begged for an explanation.

Ronan smirked, taking a step closer.

I flinched.

"Hell didn't want me," He growled the snarky reply, the smooth voice tattering slightly as if he was trying to sound *worse* than he truly was. His movements were fluid, too perfect, like his feet weren't touching the floor, but he was levitating ever so slightly above the ground.

"I'm your guest. We established this, yes?" he asked, and a flutter of heated anger washed over my entire body.

"You are not a guest," I snapped, taking another step back.

"You are a parasite."

His expression shifted slightly, his eyes narrowing.

"Do you always touch yourself while thinking intimately of *parasites?*"

My face flushed again with embarrassment.

My trap.

I swallowed hard, buying myself a moment to think.

I had an idea.

I slowly stepped back again, moving deeper into the bedroom where I had once armed myself with holy water and sage—the leftovers from my failed experiment.

"So you *were* watching me?" I let a sly smile show in my expression.

"How could I not? You placed my face directly at your bedside."

"You're disgusting," I mouthed, still with a smile.

"Yet, you can't seem to look away."

I refused to give him another reaction. I slowly reached for the bottle, stretching slightly, but it was still too far away.

"You're a shadow, a trick of light. Whatever you are, you don't belong here." I snapped at him with a fury I didn't know was inside me.

"And yet, here I am," he said, spreading his arms slightly. He reached out and flicked the light switch, and the room darkened.

"Capable of interacting with your interesting world, my, my— so much has changed." His grin widened, and slowly, his human features became more focused, revealing an incredible man.

A jawline chiseled out of stone. Lips you'd want to have pressed against *every* surface of your body. Eyes of gold that could pull your secrets from your mouth without trying. Shoulders and arms that could lift you effortlessly into his arms.

My lips parted slightly while I considered what kind of man he might have once been, but his words pierced through the inappropriate daydream.

"Doesn't it make you curious, Wren Rivers?"

The sound of my name sent a shiver down my spine. I hated how it sounded—perfectly placed on his velvet lips as if he was meant to whisper it for all eternity.

"What do you want?" I demanded, pausing my reach for the bottle of his soon-to-be undoing.

His gaze darkened, and for a brief moment, something flickered across his face—sadness.

"I want... what I've always wanted. To feel. To live."

I blinked, caught off guard by the sudden vulnerability in his voice.

"Wha—" I paused, "What?" I questioned, shocked.

He stepped closer, the playful edge in his tone softening. "I've been trapped in the canvas for centuries. Watching the world pass by, owner after owner, life after life." His eyes passed to the now empty portrait canvas.

"But never living it myself. Do you know what that's like? To be forgotten, passed around like an object? To exist, but never truly be?"

His façade was crumbling, his bravado and mischievous play faded. He was made of something raw and aching. A tortured soul undone by his circumstances, he and I... not so different.

Just from different worlds.

I stopped reaching for the holy water.

"I don't—" I couldn't finish my response.

He held his stare, wildly deepening into my eyes. The golden flecks of amber trying to pull my secrets from me.

"Wren, *Little Bird*, you are different." He began to move closer. "You saw something in my portrait, didn't you?" His mouth mere inches from my face, "And you reached for me."

He sighed, "An alike soul, a flicker of recognition and—" He paused and stepped slightly closer, "hope."

I didn't think I wanted to know any more about Ronan. How was I so tortured? How was I so... broken? How did he think I related to a ghost from the 1600s that's been mercilessly trapped inside a painting, forced to endure centuries of a passing life but unable to *interact*?

We were *not* alike. That couldn't be true. I *lived* my life so much that my demons chased me into this God-forsaken house. I lived so hard that my heart had been torn and shattered by good-for-nothing men.

But...

I also lived through the lens of a camera, afraid to experience anything and *miss* it. I sighed, staring my own demons directly in their face.

"But you're wasting a life I almost had." He sneered, his vulnerability faded in his words that cut through me like a well-sharpened knife.

The tension returned and swallowed the moment whole. Every instinct in my body screamed at me to run and grab the holy water. I didn't want to hear whatever he was about to say next.

Toss it, and run. I thought to myself.

But despite everything, despite the incessant screaming in my mind and the queasy feeling in my gut, I couldn't convince myself to move.

Something about him intrigued me.

I hated it.

I hated *him.*

But why did he think we were the same?

Wasting my life?

But without another second *wasted*, I grabbed the holy water and tossed it onto him. I did it.

I killed the ghost.

***

A slow, wicked smile spread across his face as if nothing had happened. The holy water had no effect. Ronan stood firm, his only movement the subtle blinks of his eyes. The water seamlessly dribbled off him and slowly tapped against the wood floor before completely evaporating.

I squared my shoulders, doubling down on my decision. Ghost, revenant, specter, phantom—I'd vanquish him here, now. No sob story, melancholy, or story weaved with endless sorrow would spin me. I wanted him *disintegrated.*

I grabbed for the sage and lit it… I hadn't read the instructions, so I twirled it around me in a protective barrier and waved it maniacally toward Ronan. Ensuring that the smoke's fingers reached him, clawing at him in a way I wouldn't dare.

"You—you think you can just haunt me forever?" I panted, "Ruin my life until I *give in?*"

"Isn't that what you really want, Wren?" He asked directly.

"Where did you get that idea?" I dropped the sage to my side. Its billowing smoke twirling around the room in tendrils of an otherworldly nature, a spectacle that would have usually attracted my attention. But, my frustrations with my invading ghost were growing deeper—angrier and took an overwhelming priority of the beauty of the moment.

"Your endless string of empty lovers, your unfulfilled career, this empty home with no love for yourself or anyone else." He smirked at me, and began pacing around me like it were a dance. "This couldn't be what you fight so hard for?" He stepped toward me, no longer saturated by the water I'd doused him in.

Dry, warm, sizzling with a heat that made me gasp.

"Your life is your own, but it's empty and one of solace and sadness." He reached out, and I flinched, prepared for him to end me.

He pulled my chin up, "But you are a Wren," he smiled, and my knees started to buckle under me.

"A songbird," He brushed a stray lock of hair from my face, and all the hate I'd built inside melted away with his touch. It wasn't human, but it wasn't haunting. It was fulfilling, captivating… enthralling like he was a love spell that had been cast upon me. My willingness to fight the magic subsided, and I relinquished my control.

"You mustn't *want* this life you've been given if you'd squander it so," he whispered. "But Ronan Arslane can show you how to *live* it."

"*Ronan Arslane.*" I whimpered his name delicately, unsure if it was a curse or a prayer, as he brought my face up to his.

His smirk deepened as he chuffed.

"Get. Out." I cried, a single tear slipped free—a traitor, hot and unforgiving. It sliced down my cheek, searing into my skin like a knife, its pain declaring that it belonged to him.

My face was stuck planted in his hands. He cupped it with such tenderness, but my body revolved in such hate and anger. I felt it rumbling in my chest. It pushed out my breaths erratically and made me feel unhinged and disconnected.

How had he read me like this?

How had he cracked open my heart and *invaded* its contents? The secrets I kept buried even from myself—the fears I'd never expressed to anyone, not even my closest friends.

Ronan Arslane was the devil, and I was going to destroy him.

♫ "Take Me To Church" – Hozier

CHAPTER 6

Death

The looming responsibility of my career could no longer be avoided. I had photos due for several larger clients and meetings to set for some prospective new clients.

My house was a work of art. It was an alluring place with perfect lighting and tall, glamorous gallery walls. I wanted to invite potential clients to my studio to see my gallery of portraits and discuss formatting and inspiration. However, the spare bedroom, my editing studio, was a graveyard made up of discarded relics from a version of me that hadn't survived my reawakening. The boxes were now caskets containing trinkets and clutter from a life that no longer had existed.

It felt like ages.

But it had only been months.

There was a heaviness about my day, which made finding motivation rather difficult. I wished for a moment... that motivation grew on trees like apples, and I could just pick a few for just enough momentum to... *start.*

The weight, that heaviness—It felt like a truth I'd been avoiding. Ronan had shattered my heart when he'd made me face it without warning. I *had* lived a string of unfulfilling events. He wasn't wrong. In fact, his accuracy felt like an arrow straight into my chest.

I had been letting things happen to me instead of making my own way. My failures were always someone else's fault or 'my bad luck'—an excuse I let myself believe over the truth far too often.

But now, I didn't want a ghost who haunted me with my own demons to be something that *happened* to me. I wanted to defeat it. I wanted to overpower whatever insanity this was and send it back to the dark, dank hole from which it had crawled from.

And, to start...

I had to dispose of the life that made me this way, including the useless things I'd acquired.

A chilling breeze drifted over me, raising my skin to a prickle. I maintained my stance—my hands planted firmly on my hips, surveying the work I had cut out for myself. I let the anxiety of clearing this office quickly overwhelm me. It felt like a cloud filled to the brim and ready to burst with rain.

Sometimes, rain was cleansing.

If I hadn't been so focused on destroying Ronan, maybe my responsibilities wouldn't have grown into their own kind of haunting. Each box and task took longer than I'd ever imagined. I felt stuck in purgatory—a room full of endless boxes of the remnants of an old life, but every time you cleared one, three more took their place.

There was something *off* in this room today. Something that didn't feel quite right about it. I'd felt Ronan's chilling signature when I'd started. He was here, watching me problem-solve my way out of whatever this was... A trap, a trick—some magical testament he was putting me through.

After I'd moved the first three boxes, it hit me.

Ronan used whatever magic he had to weigh these boxes down *purposefully*. I lifted what should have been a seemingly weightless box, filled with throws and fabrics I once had strewn about my apartment for "texture."

And, it weighed what a box of bricks should.

Ronan was the devil behind this entrapment. He was quite literally boxing me in. I recognized manipulation when I saw it. It was another way to stop me from pushing past his insults and growing from my mistakes.

I made every attempt to let this be another one of his games where his futile attempts rolled off my back. I tried to chuckle, to laugh it off.

But it triggered me.

A snapping inside the dam that held back my overflowing anger. It started as a crack, but as I let the realization that he was watching me suffer through cleaning my life, the crack expanded, and my anger came rushing into my body like a tsunami.

Was this a minor inconvenience? *Yes.*

Did I let it rip through me like it was something worse? Also, *yes.*

The emotional onslaught tore through my entire body as the tears flowed out, unstoppable like the tides of a raging sea. I slumped down against the wall with the box of fabrics planted between my legs. I pressed myself against it, knowing it wouldn't slide. It was an immovable boulder.

My hot tears seared my cool skin as they plummeted toward the ground. I wiped my face with my sleeve, but let them fall where they desired. There was no use hiding my sorrow, not anymore.

My heart stung, and my frustrations pounded, pulling my entire body along and causing me to sink into the inescapable hole of anger.

"Your life is your own, but it's empty and one of solace and sadness."

Ronan's selfish words rang in my ears as tears flowed freely from my eyes. I wasn't *squandering* my life. I was making the best out of a series of bad and overwhelming shitty situations.

This house was supposed to be *mine.* Ronan Arslane was ruining it. After Evan, I fled *here.* This was my castle, my solace, a place where I could finally be safe.

And this—whatever Ronan was doing—was not *safe.*

Suddenly, an idea struck me. Perhaps it was just the box that was heavy, the container that held everything together. I slowly lifted one of the textiles from the box. It was its normal weight. I reached in, grabbed an armful, and tossed them down the stairs without a second thought.

"Fuck you, Ronan," I whispered as I watched the flighty fabrics float down the stairs as if the wind caught them and asked them to dance on their way down.

I could feel when he'd settled his gaze on me, a chilling reminder that I was never alone, that I hadn't yet defeated my demon. Coming face to face with the reality that my life was a sad string of nothing was only the beginning.

Ronan wouldn't let me forget that I had a life he would kill to live. *I needed to figure out what Ronan was truly made of.* But while I was researching him, I could feel that I, too, was being intently studied.

I stepped down the stairs, sweeping the mess I'd made with the breeze of my momentum. I caught him in the corner of my eye.

"You need a new hobby," I muttered, folding one of the larger blankets and tossing it onto the couch.

"There's a thing called Chess now. Perhaps you've heard of it?" I snickered and arched my eyebrow at the shape that was as quick-moving as an elusive shadow.

"Creeping around and staring at me is not as charming as you believe," I added.

"Chess is older than you and I, Wren," He replied, his voice laden with intent. "Delight me in conversation, Little Bird, would you rather be a pawn or a Queen?"

His voice tickled down the back of my neck. He was close. His breath wasn't warm. It was cold, like a winter night up North.

"It's the twenty-first century. We don't have *Queens* anymore." I rolled my eyes. "We're all pawns, now." I let the cynicism slither off my tongue.

"Do you always let the world tell you who you are?" Ronan asked with a certainty that I knew would lead to a conversation I wasn't emotionally equipped to handle.

"No, I just don't play games, and pretending to be a Queen in a world of working professionals is borderline insane," I paused and let the thought linger, "No—it's actual insanity."

His shape stormed me, stopping mere inches from my face. He reached out with his long, dark fingers and lifted my chin. I was paralyzed from making any quick movements.

I was in a trance or scared stiff.

My heart hadn't caught up to how quick Ronan was. He was like lightning when he was agitated. His only move was to scatter your thoughts or knock you off your game. Ronan Arslane was nothing but a jump-scare *monster*.

"Wren, you *are* a queen. The world doesn't tell you what you are. You tell the world what you are. " His velvety smooth voice made me hesitate with a curious fear.

"Okay then," I whispered back, my face still close to his, "Then I am an almighty ghost vanquisher, and... you're next," I grinned as Ronan dissipated into nothing, leaving a misty chill in his place.

"Go ahead, Little Bird. Many have tried, none have succeeded," A voice without a shape whispered into the air and twisted around before releasing the tension in the room.

***

Ivy: Found some interesting stuff about your painting.

Ivy: You free?

I wiped my forehead with my arm and gently set the knife I'd been using to chop vegetables on the counter. I flipped my towel onto my shoulder, tapping the green 'call' button as quickly as possible.

"That was fast." Her voice was not quite as peppy as it usually is. I pinned the phone between my shoulder and my ear and resumed cooking.

"Babe, your painting... it ain't looking good," she said hesitantly. "You ready for this?"

I set the knife down again—a precaution. It was better for everyone that I didn't have any weapons handy if this news was bad.

"V, pretty much nothing surprises me anymore. Hit me," I said, and braced myself against the counter.

"The painting dates back to the late 1500s, according to what I found, so that part of the auction details were true," Ivy began. "It belonged to a woman named Isolde Wyld—a painter and, according to a few reliable sources, a witch. She was known for these dark, haunting portraits. The part, the scary part?" Ivy didn't stop. She continued, "Almost every one of her subjects disappeared shortly after being painted."

A chill ran down my spine. "Disappeared?"

"Yeah, Ivy confirmed. "The rumor is that she trapped them in the paintings, cursed canvases, folklore territory, but still creepy as hell."

"How many *people* did she paint, my *God?*"

"Thousands of people have Wyld paintings hanging in their homes. They're like a creepy, highly sought-after heirloom."

"That's morbid, Ivy," I whispered.

I glanced toward the stairs, where I knew the painting was still stuck to my wall, unmovable by any earthly force.

"And the man in *my* painting?"

"That's where the trail goes cold," Ivy said. "I couldn't find much about him, but there's speculation that he was someone close to Isolde—maybe even her lover." She caught her breath, "The bits and pieces I've stitched together say that he was her greatest masterpiece... and her greatest curse."

The words oddly stung me.

An ex-lover had cursed Ronan. It hit too close to home. He wasn't so perfect after all. *Mr. 'Come with me if you want to live'* hadn't done himself any favors when he was alive. But, perhaps, I'd be willing to admit that we *weren't* so different.

"Thanks, Ivy," I said, my voice quieter.

"I'll keep digging. Maybe we can de-curse it, and it can just be a weird painting and a funny story."

"So, like holy water and sage?"

"Oh no, girl, you need firepower. Like a whole pentagram and some pillar candles and what sounds like a demonic chant."

"Sounds like a really fun girl's night, V," I teased.

Ivy let out a sigh. "Be careful, okay?" Ivy's tone shifted, "This stuff is... I'm not reading great stories. There's a reason no one outbid you. It's intense. Maybe even a little dangerous."

"I will," I promised, ending the call.

✳✳✳

I approached the painting after dinner. I'd spent my entire meal contemplating and planning what would happen next.

Ronan was a victim and also an uninvited guest in my home. The two could be true, but his tragic start isn't a cause for my accommodation.

But maybe—just maybe, there was a deal to strike. Perhaps I could donate him somewhere where he'd be more useful. I envisioned a haunted house that makes its money off the scares.

Or, his historical relevance could score him a prime location in a busy museum, where he would have the entire world and its history at his disposal. If Ronan had a desperate thirst for knowledge, a museum would tickle his fancy.

The fact that I was bargaining with myself, trying to seek an alternative to completely destroying Ronan, meant that I was turning a page on whether or not I hated my ghost.

I needed to strike an even balance, *something* slightly less intense than exorcising a demon who'd lived centuries.

A question repeating over and over in my mind...

Why did it have to be me who ended his reign?

Someone else could do it.

But I ultimately decided I'd possibly give Ronan his first *human* decision.

✳✳✳

"So," I crossed my arms, as I tended to do when talking to a wall laden with old art. It was the only sensible mannerism in conversations of this nature.

"Care to explain how you ended up in a painting?"

The silence lingered.

"How exactly did *Isolde* trap you in there?" I asked again, letting her name tickle the air in a way I knew would hit Ronan in his darkest place. Suddenly, for the first time, I witnessed the paint of the portrait ripple and tear on the canvas.

It pulled and stretched, and from the darkness of the frame, Ronan peeled himself off of his primary stage and manifested into my room as if stepping through a portal. His darkness overtook the room, commanding the shadows and light to build his blurred form.

He stood solid in the center of the room, owning his existence. His expression was one full of anguish and pain. "Don't ever say her name," he threatened me. His tone was deep and slow. His threat felt full of intent, like a promise he'd enjoy keeping.

"My, Ronan, have I struck a nerve? You don't *like* the name of the witch that took your precious life away?" I let out a little cackle at how easily the discovery had triggered him. The phantom who claimed to know my soul as if it were his own had a secret, and I was willing to exploit it.

Just like he'd done mine.

I finally dug up something I could enjoy using to terrorize his heart. It wasn't lost on me that I was antagonizing an ancient spirit just after telling my best friend I'd be careful. I was a dirty little liar, and it felt good.

"Isolde," I whispered in a direct attack. I was not mincing my words, and I was not being coy or cute. I wanted Ronan to suffer as he'd made me for these last weeks.

I had said Isolde's name with intentional cruelty.

I felt Ronan's entire body slam against mine, and together, we met the strength of two-hundred-year-old plaster and slat board on brick block. Dust plumed behind me as my entire body slammed firmly against the wall with a bone-snapping thud.

The wall splintered behind us, the cracks and snaps of the building materials masking the noise of my bones fracturing inside my body. I felt the pain of the impact shoot up my spine and radiate in both directions toward my hips and my arms, down to my fingertips.

A tingling sensation that turned bad.

As I realized what had happened, Ronan pressed his magic against me and crushed me against the wall, perhaps forgetting I was a mere human. Or perhaps not.

It had seemed that I'd angered him.

Ronan pushed against me mercilessly, his hands tightening around my throat. I was terrified but oddly comforted by his aggression toward me. Our hate was mutual. I understood our dynamic—he wanted me dead, and I wanted him destroyed, too.

I met his use of deadly force with a haunting smile, for I was powerless against whatever strength his magic gave him. He was a magical force that my muscles cowered against. I was paralyzed in my body, but this smile... It was all I had to fight against his violence.

"Do it, Ronan," I whispered, barely getting the words through my rapidly closing throat. He held me in place like I hadn't ever been in this position before... like someone else hadn't harnessed their hate for me and tried to snuff out the light in my eyes.

They had. I was no stranger to being on the edge of death, with a demon's hands choking my life from me.

"*Please.*" Tears formed in my eyes, and my vision blurred under them. I could feel my life closing out. I experienced overwhelming peace as the darkness washed over my body, causing me to lose all feeling.

The nothingness I had pretended didn't exist—had always been waiting. I had spent so long running from it, but here, wrapped in his hands, it felt almost... welcoming. No more failure. No more regrets. No more trying. This was peace.

This was the death of Wren Rivers.

♫ "Everything Sucks" – Vaultboy

CHAPTER 7

Monsters

Evan was a demon in his own right.

He was an artist like me, but his form was painting his beautiful lies like classic masterpieces. He sang sweet poems of fibs and belted out ballads of make-believe.

Evan was married with two children and a golden retriever.
And engaged to me.

An investment banker who was bored with his missionary-style wife, farmer's markets, and cocktail hours. He stumbled into open-mic night at Sam, Ivy, and my favorite dive. Despite being woefully out of place there, he approached me with a suave confidence that I was all too eager to accept as truth.

He said all of the right things, and his swagger was undeniable.

After a while, it became clear that I was just his temporary high. His high-risk, high-reward investment. I gave all of myself to him because I thought he was edgy and alpha. I didn't doubt that this was the man I was supposed to *marry*.

On paper, we were a match made in heaven. His high-anxiety job in finance blended well with the slow pace of his smooth-as-honey artist *mistress*.

He stopped me from buzzing around the city with a camera in hand, waiting to catch the moment of a lifetime, but instead forced me beside him as a trophy to flash around his partners and subordinates at work. He held his love over my head and only tossed me scraps of affection when I performed for him.

Evan had an allure about him that made you look past it all. His perfect smile, ice blue eyes, manicured nails, and a sleek, empty, high-dollar penthouse apartment—all part of an elaborate disguise.

He used these very real things to confirm his lies to me, to paint them as realities, and he manipulated me into believing every serene whisper of our future. Over time, he tore me from meaningful friendships and ripped apart my career success piece by piece by making me question my talent and turn down clients who might endanger the false world he'd created.

And when I wasn't looking, he was fucking anything that walked, too.

On a perfect day at the park—85 degrees and sunny, not a cloud in the sky. A bold private investigator approached me and revealed that the life I'd known, the life I'd been living with my *fiancé*, was all a lie.

Evan's wife had hired him, the investigator, and sent him to inform me. I suppose I wouldn't want to come face to face with my husband's mistress either. So, she decided that having him break my heart into a thousand pieces in a park was the best idea.

I accepted the photographs with a polite nod, since that was what you did when your entire world collapsed in public.

And just like that, the bright and sunny day didn't make sense anymore, and I wished that it matched the condition of my heart. Hailing, thrashing the trees around like the outer edges of a hurricane. But the sun prevailed, and the forecast hadn't changed.

Evan's wife, *Sarah*, knew I didn't know about her, and maybe she felt bad for me and sent this man as a messenger, a hero, or a peace offering.

Perhaps she truly felt bad that her treacherous husband's lies had the strength and momentum to break four hearts simultaneously.

Because I'm sure the dog didn't even like him.

I knew that my world was being tossed upside down. I knew that my life, as I'd known it before that moment, would drastically change. I knew I might be different from that moment on, but there was a sliver, a tiny microscopic, flittering speck that was *grateful* it was over.

Evan was hurting me, and I thought it was *our thing*. I thought the moments of tension-filled violence were our cat-and-mouse game. I thought I was *submissive* to a strong man.

But... that wasn't at all what I'd agreed to. I didn't agree to black eyes and nearly broken bones. I didn't agree to be a punching bag for Evan to release the day's stresses. And I was relieved that I wouldn't have to be anymore.

I confronted him. Against my better judgment...

Our last night ended in a whirlwind of violence, police lights, a restraining order, and my name in the papers despite being promised protection from such public humiliation.

I hadn't talked much about *how* it ended, only that it just had. And I can't say I was entirely innocent, but Evan's fists slamming into my body until I was unconscious was something I didn't think I deserved, no matter what words I'd said before it.

Sam and Ivy tried to warn me, but I ignored their good sense too many times. They had started withdrawing from parts of my life he had crossed into. The dinner invitations and game nights dwindled from an every-weekend event to only special occasions. I missed so much of their lives and accomplishments because I played my dutiful role as an unknowing, naïve *homewrecker*.

Evan *hated* Ivy. They were like oil and vinegar—no, that would at least leave a palatable taste in your mouth. They were fire and gasoline, and they left *nothing* in their wake.

Ivy... God, she's no-nonsense and straight to the point. Evan's entire personality was bullshit, a falsified narrative, and Ivy ate up how—*well*, dumb he was.

Ivy, though, is *something else*. Her intelligence—her ability to notice things other people don't see. She's not normal, and she's never been. I can't put my finger on it, but Ivy has always felt magical—powerful, like a force you wouldn't want to step in front of.

I remember telling her once that her superpower was being a best friend. I guess I had an Ivy in all the darkness and brutality of the world. So, maybe life wasn't always so unfair.

I'd only learned how much hate he had in his heart on that last night. The names he'd called her, the vicious insults he slung at her, I felt as if they were my own. My heart broke with each crack of his whip-like tongue at her expense.

I had thrown a glass at his head before he'd even mentioned Sam. Sam was sacred, and a line neither Ivy nor I would ever let anyone outside our circle cross.

I didn't think. My hand just moved. One second, I was standing there, letting his voice crawl over me like oil, and the next, my fingers were wrapped around the nearest glass. I threw it—hard. It met the wall with a force, shattering just beside his head, spraying shards across his expensive shirt.

His lip curled into something unholy. His eyes—blackened.

"You little bitch, I'll *kill you*," he murmured.

And I believed him.

After the chaos had settled—sitting alone in my apartment wasn't a choice I wanted to make. I showed up unannounced at Ivy's apartment, defeated, my wrist and arm broken, my neck marred and bruised, but my body no more broken than my heart and my ego.

The way her face crumpled at the scrapes and cuts. She delicately bandaged what she could—wrapped and iced my swollen parts. She covered my neck with a silk scarf of the most beautiful blend of watercolors, turning the bruises into something easier to understand.

We sat together in complete silence, as there weren't any words I needed to hear that Ivy hadn't already said to me before. I replayed them in my head, trying to locate the exact moment I should have listened to her and Sam. Trying to pinpoint the moment that I regretted the most.

Was it when Evan proposed with the breathtaking cushion-cut diamond of manipulation wrapped in a halo of smaller sparkling emerald lies?

Was it when his co-worker had called me 'Sarah' at happy hour?

Was it when he gave me a black eye later that night for asking who 'Sarah' even was?

Ivy was *not* the one to tell me that she told me so. She knew better than that. I was already humiliated and shamed. I felt less than broken, as if I didn't actually exist anymore. Any identity that I once had—gone. Evan had consumed it and claimed it as his own. He only allowed me to feel what he'd decided I should.

Maybe I didn't deserve the happy-ever-after.

While Evan might have ruined me for anyone ever again, It was *Marshall* who left the door open for him to do it.

Three weeks after my mom's cancer diagnosis—stage 2. He packed his stuff out of our apartment under the cover of darkness and left without saying anything. It seemed he'd vanished into thin air, not the only ghost in my life ever to haunt me.

It was a Tuesday morning when I realized it. The bed was cold, and his toothbrush was missing from the holder. His favorite mug—the one he hated when I used—was gone from the drying rack.

I texted him. No response.

I called him. No voicemail.

I checked our lease—his name had been removed.

The whole time, I had been waiting for a breakup. But what did I get instead?

A fucking vanishing act.

In those tiny wisps and moments just before you fall asleep, I'd remember it had happened, and I relived the humiliation all over again, every gripping moment of it.

The problem with my relationship with Marshall was that I ignored all the signs leading up to his departure. I'd pretended I was fulfilled and that Marshall made me happy.

In hindsight, Marshall had worn me down and grated off parts of me I once loved. I'd developed a short fuse, exploding erratically at Ivy over something slight. I'd sharpened my tongue against Sam's never-ending, unserious conversation. I would wake up overstimulated, and as the day went on, it would only get worse until I was a menace to be around.

I remember coming home from a studio shoot with an up-and-coming author named Taylor Halethorpe. I was excited about how my shots came out and couldn't wait to tell Marshall about my day.

I wasn't often giddy about something that happened with my clients, so this felt special.

As soon as I walked through the door, he stood and crowded me with the intricate details of his day. I became overwhelmed within minutes. Marshall was an engineer, so much of his work involved complex thoughts and understandings. I tried to let him indulge a little—I gave him the space and did my best listening.

But when he was finished, and I had held onto my excitement for so long, I opened my mouth to share, and he fled the room, uninterested in anything I had to say. I'd spent the day with a famous author, a writer of brilliant books and stories, and he couldn't be bothered even to feign interest for more than thirty seconds.

Resentment piled up when each day consisted of the same undermining behavior. Marshall never acknowledged that he was emotionally selfish in our relationship. He was completely blind to how he consumed all the energy in the room, like a giant black hole.

And, *God damn,* he talked way too much.

He was always talking.

I often wondered how one person could have so much to say when they were so *uninteresting.* Marshall had no hobbies or passions. His friends weren't friends the way Ivy, Sam, and I were. They weren't intimately involved in the details of his life.

Sometimes, I'd even stand in the bathroom and stare psychotically at the blank, boring, unpainted wall so that he'd have to take a pause. So that I could hear the bliss of a silent room.

Even then, I swore I heard him still chattering away to himself when I wasn't in the room.

We went through the motions of a young, new couple, but they were hollow things. The only fire we experienced was when we'd both had a little too much to drink and would sneak into an obscure bathroom to fuck. The thrill of being caught was the only thing that motivated us to touch each other.

When big life decisions, *like new jobs*, were presented, we had nothing in common. Nothing held us together—at least, not the way real love holds people together. We were certainly not held together by the lease with both of our names.

The most statistically perfect relationships may look sturdy from a distance, but throw in a sprinkle of real life, and they could come crashing down if there isn't some chaos-driven passion solidified into a foundation.

Your love had to be a little crazy to make it through the chaos of real life. There is a love out there that does that for people, you know. There's a love out there that drops you to your knees and makes you worship the ground they walk on. That makes them consume every inch of your mind and soul. There's love that makes you want to keep it all a secret and hold it close and never let it go, for it's rare. It's special. And it's only yours.

But what did I even know of love like that? I'd only seen it as it was supposed to be in movies and love stories—but even that was becoming grossly tainted with the amount of smut I'd been reading.

Between the humiliation and the betrayals, I eventually became an empty shell, a husk. I filled my nights with strange men, letting them waste my time in the dark corners of bars where no one would recognize me. I'd tell them different names and jobs and invent entire backstories. I'd answer every question with a lie—they didn't care what I did for a living.

All they wanted to know was where I lived.

Was it close enough to walk?

And how few clothes would we be wearing when we got there?

Some even dared to think they could *stay* until the sun came up. But as soon as I had taken from them what I'd wanted. I'd toss them their stuff and stare blankly while they left, pretending that these empty nights didn't make me feel more hollow and less like a human.

I'd masked the emptiness of these engagements as control. I thought it meant I knew what I was doing... but was careless.

With a sigh of relief, I let their names fade into the darkness, forgetting them as quickly as they came, which was always rather *quickly.*

I concealed most of this from Ivy and Sam—they hadn't known the monster I'd descended into, but they hadn't asked. It was clear that either my best friends avoided telling me I was a ticking time bomb, or I had learned to lie from being so close to some of the greats.

But if we're still counting, the best boyfriend I'd ever had was for six hours before he came out of the closet. *Sam.*

God, I missed Sam. The only man I have ever really trusted. The only one who never asked for more than I could give. And the only one who would never, *ever* be mine. And that was completely fine.

Suppose I had to live with Sam or the ghost that had killed me. I would choose the ghost.

And maybe that says more about me than I wanted to admit.

♫ "WITHOUT YOU" – The Kid LAROI

CHAPTER 8

Answers

My eyes opened, and I was buried in bed under a mountain of blankets.

I didn't move. I barely breathed.

The thought struck like lightning.

I should be dead.

Was this heaven?

Ronan had killed me. I remembered the snap of my spine against the wall, the force of his rage slamming into me. I had heard my brittle bones break under the strength and pressure of the maddened specter. His hands tightened around my throat until the world faded into a vast nothing.

I was sure that I felt the rapid fire of my heart stop completely.

Why was I waking up?

I tried to move, a light wiggle of my fingers—but a shooting pain lanced up my arm, ripping my half-awakened daze away from me and sending me into full awareness.

Everything hurt. My ribs ached, and my throat throbbed as if it had its own heartbeat. My spine had deep, twisting pain that embedded itself deeply into my body. I wish I had died because this was excruciating. I silently begged, offering my tears as sacrifice, for God or the Devil to take me quickly.

I'd try again in the next one.

I'd conceded. I had surrendered to the magnetic pull and the enticing draw of ending it all, but I was still here. Perhaps because I *wanted* it, it was kept from me. Maybe... because I'd begged him to end my curse, he let it continue. Anything not to give Wren what she desired.

Agonizing pains vibrated my bones with each movement, no matter how small or insignificant I tried to make them. They remembered the violence, the memory of the trauma lingering in them like nightmares.

I cried out, panting and groaning while I slowly crawled from the burrow of warmth I'd created for myself in the cold room. I gently ran my hands down my body, feeling each part with a sensitive touch, ensuring that I was, in fact, whole.

I winced each time my fingertips passed over my chest and neck. I paused my hand delicately for a moment and felt the thudding of my beating heart. Whole, pumping blood to all of my vital organs, but not left unbroken.

I pulled myself into gravity's embrace, and against the warning signs of pain panging against me, I slowly limped my way toward the tub, grabbing anything that might stop me from toppling over and onto the floor.

However, a fall to my knees seemed inescapable. It wasn't slow, but I felt like I'd fallen in slow motion, as if I was lightly placed on the floor and the wind had caught me and cradled me to the ground.

A reach.

A stretch.

There was a scream of undeniable brokenness before I was finally met with that familiar reply. The groan of the old pipes sang a sweet song of relief when I swirled the brass handle, and the steam of searing warmth shot out into the cool porcelain.

I needed to be coddled, held, and embraced by something far warmer than death. I needed to let this body simmer in the warmth of a healing pond of water. I needed a moment to catch my breath and understand I was alive.

While I'd surrendered to my fate, a knowing had taken over a part of my mind. It wasn't until the darkness covered my vision and the last thoughts of my life flashed before me that I realized I had made a harrowing mistake.

I'd miscalculated something.

I didn't *want* to die.

No, I did not. I wanted to *live*.

I felt regret and a pang of hopelessness at the very last moment. I stared death, quite literally, in the face and laughed at it as if I had nothing to lose. But...

I did.

I had Ivy and Sam, and I had my art and photography. I had this house and my family.

A pang of regret for not calling them enough.

I had a whole, *free* life ahead of me that I couldn't wait to fill with friends and family and memories of what it truly means to be alive.

I had miscalculated.

Just before I'd lowered myself into the vessel, preparing to sear my skin from my body and convince my muscles to learn to move once again, I noticed the bruises. The marks flashed back at me from the large antique mirror. The rest of my body blurred and unfocused, but the darkened spaces of my battered body were bright and bold.

My neck was covered in a purple darkness from the attempt on my life. It hadn't been a nightmare that I'd endured—no. Ronan nearly killed me, or he had, and his magic had brought me back from my death.

Reminders that Ronan had tried to take the sacred magic of life from me. I thought it all a bad nightmare with a physical manifestation, a magic that hadn't yet worn off. I thought it was an illusion of death to push me *in line*. But his harm had been real. It had all been so *very* real.

These marks on my body proved it.

And I hated him for it.

I hated that I felt, again, like a battered woman.

I felt my mind spiral, bringing back a string of memories I'd thought I'd force down and away. Memories that I thought were buried under the foundation of my fresh start. But all along, they were sitting on the surface, and Ronan, he'd strangled them out of me. My body recoiled in a panic as if it knew Ronan might do it again.

Perhaps Ronan was unaware that I'd survived, and he'd come back to finish what he'd started. Maybe he wasn't done torturing me, breaking me.

I wished I were afraid, but I had no energy to fear. I was wasted, my soul spread too thin to fear that which would behave so cowardly.

I whispered a name, and he believed that for such a crime, I deserved death? He murdered me, and since his portrait still hung above my mantel, he continued to take up space in a home that wasn't his own. In a place where he was unwelcome.

I sank deep into the tub, letting the warmth wash the moment from me, letting myself become unburdened by the danger of this demon that now wanted me dead more than once. I closed my eyes and caught a flash of a memory. Ronan's carrying me to bed.

I couldn't confirm it was real, perhaps a manifestation of a deep desire that will never be.

The realization that a small part of me wanted a savior left a powerfully disgusting taste in my mouth. I rubbed my tongue around, trying to make it disappear, but the sourness tingled.

"If I wanted you dead, I would have already devoured your soul, and no one would ever come to know of your fate."

A demonic chuckle followed his empty threat.

His words pierced the calm I'd created in the bathroom, darting through my introspection like an arrow let loose from a bow only yards from where I lay. He was closer than I thought.

"Well, you've clearly never met Ivy Holloway," I whispered.

"Wren, perhaps I had to break you so you could find a way to *live*," Ronan replied. It seemed like he genuinely believed the insanity of what he was saying.

"Ronan—Fuck you." He was becoming predictable, slithering himself into my most intimate moments with threats of vicious violence.

"Not yet, Little Bird." His voice pulled into the tone of a smile, and when I closed my eyes, I could see him. The deadly flecks of gold scattered in his eyes. I could see his sharp jawline and his delicious but poisonous smile. His dark hair was slicked back.

"But soon, you'll beg for it."

I plunged my entire body under the water and held myself there until the air I'd taken with me turned bad, and my body betrayed my wildest wishes to stay submerged.

Ronan Arslane was nothing more than a revolting curse—a shameful haunt. A pathetic excuse for a nightmare, and I... would end him.

✷✷✷

A week after I had pronounced myself dead, I took my first client meeting in my new gallery and editing office. The house was picture-perfect. Every piece of art and furniture was placed appropriately, and my gallery books were on the table in the living room. I curated every color I painted and hand-selected every piece of art that spoke with a deeper voice.

Pun intended.

I met the prospective client at the door, and as he entered, he, too, felt what I felt when I saw this house for the first time: the awe of history and appreciation for the details that Victorian houses had. It was a work of art and evidence that two hundred years ago, builders were artists, too.

"They don't make them like this anymore," the young man said, adjusting his tie as he glanced around at the subtle, time-accurate décor.

"No, I certainly got lucky with this one. It's cozy," I smiled and brushed my hand over the patterned silk scarf I had around my neck to conceal Ronan's attempted murder. Nearly a week later, the memories of it still clung to my skin like a nightmare that wouldn't end.

"Come, Mr. Ashford, let me show you my gallery—this way." We slowly ascended the beautiful wooden stairs with the ornate rail.

Together, we entered the large, newly set up gallery and modern editing suite, outfitted with full gallery walls of photos I'd taken—mostly portraits, specifically. Some were highly saturated, others were in black and white, and each one of them was special.

"Wow," he whispered as he looked at the top of the twenty-foot ceilings, every inch covered in a face I'd captured with my lenses.

"You're talented, Mrs. Rivers, what you have here, it's really quite…" he didn't finish his thought, "We'd love to work with you. We're a local non-profit, so we can't pay much." His face squinched with a little pain as he mentioned it.

"We offer photo sessions to victims of domestic violence—"

I interrupted his sentence, my head tilted. "That's an incredible gift to give someone." I paused, letting the idea flutter in my mind. "It gives them a fresh look at who they've become, a mirror of their strength—their beauty." I nodded as I connected with their mission.

"We're hoping it's a cause you can stand behind, too." But he shifted uncomfortably in his chair, and his expression alerted me to something *wrong*. That's when I realized the silk scarf had untied and was hanging from my shoulder.

We shared a knowing glance, and I grinned, "Victorian houses don't come without a few ghost kinks."

Mr. Ashford's eyes practically crossed as he choked and began to cough uncomfortably while leaning forward. "Can I get you some water? I have Iced, or Holy?" I smiled, reaching for a water bottle from the mini-fridge.

"Uhh, thank you, Mrs. Rivers," he replied, more politely than anything.

"Mr. Ashford, I'll send the contract over, and we can discuss your budget restrictions." I paused, wincing again at the sharp pain that seared through my legs from the way I'd sat down. An ironic meeting to have, domestic violence, as if the universe was trying to steer me in a direction I was fighting against.

"I'm open and willing to donate some of the services to make it work." I stood, concealing my limp, and gently shook his hand. Together, we slowly walked down the stairs back toward the majestic arched black oak front door.

Before he stepped too far from the building, he stopped on the top stair just outside the house and turned back toward me.

"I hope this isn't too forward, Mrs. Rivers,"

"Miss," I corrected him this time.

"Miss Rivers," his face blushed, "But if you ever need our services, here is my card."

His eyes met mine.

He thought *I* was a victim of *domestic* violence.

"I don't suppose you know how to exorcise ghosts, do you?"

"Not yet, Ma'am. But we can certainly find a way if that's what it takes."

He nodded at me with a half-smile.

"Thank you," I said, taking his card and looking down. Theodore Ashford," I whispered to myself.

"What a kind man." I smiled, and when I closed the door and turned, I was met with darkness—a stark contrast to the bright blue and white sky I'd just seen.

Ronan.

✳✳✳

Ronan was everywhere. No matter how much I willed it or how hard I fought against him. I cursed him with internet chants. I vanquished him with every powder, petal, and pollen I bought from internet witch doctors.

I hated him with every fiber of my being.

In a far more desperate moment, I tried to set his painting aflame on my wall, but the flame bent against its surface, refusing to ignite.

Ronan's power was witchcraft. It was blasphemy.

Unmanaged magic...

And, it was isolating.

He was shadow stretching into an existence that didn't belong to him, stretching into mine as if he owned my space.

As if he owned *me*.

He was confident and excessively indulgent, like someone who felt untouchable. His dark amusement permeated every corner of my home, making me uncomfortable and, at times, nauseous.

He watched my every move with a smirk, tilting the corners of his delicious lips. I was not only destroyed by him, but I was infatuated with every inch of him.

I daydreamed of life in 1595 alongside the real Ronan Arslane as his lover. His tall, dark, human form ravaged me repeatedly in our small cabin in the woods, where we hid from his witch, keeping our love a secret until she was hunted down and burned for her crimes.

Or in our royal palace, atop the hay of a primitive canopy bed, he—a knight—and I—a princess. My maidens secretly whispered of our escapades behind the King's back. We were the talk of the town.

His voice pierced the vivid imagery of my daydreams. Fortunately, I was convinced he couldn't yet tell what I was thinking.

"Poor Little Bird," he murmured as I sat at the kitchen table with articles about the Wyld family history, "So desperate to rid the world of me."

"Not the world, Ronan, *just my house*," I said back with a scathing tone, but I didn't look up from the screen, the reflection of death records glowing in my eyes.

I had been at it for hours, my eyes red and dry from staring intensely at the blue glow of the monitor. I had traced every path. I had followed every thread that seemed like it might lead somewhere. All roads ended. Every morsel of information I had attained was countered by something else I later learned.

He chuckled, pushing off the doorframe. He was always leaning against something. He rounded the table, and the air shifted with his smooth, ghostly movements.

"Do you really want me gone?" He leaned in close, and although I couldn't feel his breath, the implication that I might if he were human sent a crawling tickle down my spine.

You seem quite invested for someone who despises me.

"I'm invested in knowing how to be rid of you," I snapped as I turned to face him.

A mistake, immediately... a mistake.

He was closer than I realized, his face just a small space from mine. The golden light from the kitchen caught his eyes, making them glow like embers from a perpetual flame. His features became more defined each day, allowing me to see more and more of his skin, his face.

He wasn't just a shadow with only the insinuation of a man made of darkness and bent light. His transformation into someone more human drove me wild. He smelled like leather and amber and the light nostalgia of a summer day after a thunderstorm, wrapping around me, gluing itself to my mind.

"You can try," he whispered. "But you won't."

I forced myself to hold his gaze and meet his stare with equal intensity, although mine was laden with anger—a fierce, visceral anger that would have me tear him to pieces if I possessed the strength and power.

"You have a weakness, Ronan. We *all* have weaknesses."

His smile sharpened, revealing something wicked behind his eyes.

"Oh, Wren," he murmured, his voice like silk brushing against my naked body, tickling me with sin.

"Is that why you dig? Because you think you'll find something that makes me cower?" He smiled.

I hated him.

I hated how he could read me.

"Little Bird, you can look, but you won't like what you find." A flash of vulnerability crossed his expression. He may have mastered the art of reading Wren Rivers, but I was becoming the resident expert on Ronan Arslane.

I broke the gaze first, returning to my laptop and repositioning the device, refusing to let him see how his closeness had excited me. I would never let him know that deep down. I often wondered how my name would sound on the darkness of his lips, how his embrace would feel against the softest parts of my skin in the dead of night.

Looking back at my research, my eyes caught something new, something they had missed in the blur of overstimulation.

A name torn off so many other family trees.

Amelie Wyld.

A possible descendant of Isolde. My fingers hovered over the keys in delight. If Ronan was cursed into the painting by Isolde, perhaps the curse could be reversed with a descendant's power. Maybe Amelie was the key to Ronan's freedom.

I glanced up at Ronan, who stared through me into my heart.

"Find something interesting?" he drawled, leaning back against the wall behind him.

A slow smile curled my lips as I leaned back into my chair. "Maybe."

His expression remained unchanged, but I saw the flicker in his eyes—a sliver of uncertainty. He wasn't sure of the game I was playing. I let the uncomfortable silence linger between us as I now wore the smug grin of someone finally positioned for checkmate.

I couldn't remove the portrait from the wall without his help. There was only one way it could leave this house: if Ronan was willing.

"Perhaps there is a deal to be made," I said, clicking away from the screen, hiding the information for a little longer. I let the idea of freeing him linger. He didn't deserve to be free, not after *killing me.*

But maybe his curse would restore his humanity, and five hundred years of guilt would tear through his soul, leaving him lifeless *nonetheless.*

Or maybe Amelie couldn't help, but I could leave him there and run. This didn't have to end in his freedom; however, it was certainly a way to get him to agree.

He smiled but didn't say a word. The way his eyes answered me back let me know he was intrigued.

"What would you give to have your curse broken?" I asked hesitantly.

"It can't be broken. I am eternally yours, Wren Rivers, No Returns." His response was just as I had expected.

"I read that direct descendants can end curses."

"Isolde Wyld had no descendants." Ronan replied with a finality that made me question my source.

"Not quite. There is someone," I said, twirling my hair in my fingers.

"Do tell me, Wren, I can see your mind working diligently,"

"What if I took you to her?" I turned my screen toward the shadowy figure of the haunted soul. He studied the words, but his gaze was unreadable, and his composure was infuriating.

"Curious," he murmured, "You'd rather my curse broken than I destroyed?"

I flinched. The thought of vanquishing him myself had filled my mind like an obsession, but it felt impossible.

Why *had* I settled for something in the middle?

Why was I holding myself back from burning this house to the ground and taking Ronan with it?

"I just want you gone, and this feels... easier."

His smirk returned, but it wasn't as broad. It wasn't as enthusiastic.

"Then take me to her, Little Bird."

A challenge.

But I could hear the lie beneath it.

He wasn't afraid of me.

He was afraid of hope.

♫ "Omens" – UNSECRET, Neoni

CHAPTER 9

Witch Hunt

The house was nothing like I expected, yet somehow exactly as it should be. It stood, barely, on the edge of the woods, hidden by shadows and foliage that made it virtually invisible. The windows were clouded with dark dust, preventing anyone from seeing in.

Or out.

I heaved the heavy painting from the back seat into my arms, barely able to see over the top. I was unable to navigate the various shrubs and vines that were certainly placed to deter visitors.

I expected one to turn into a snake and coil around my ankle.

I shouldn't be here. I shouldn't be on a witch hunt.

But I was too far in to turn back. I was too close to getting what I'd worked so hard for—my freedom.

The door swung open before I could knock.

A tall woman with wild hair and delicate, wise eyes entered the doorway. I instantly wanted to reach for my camera and capture the bold beauty of her dark features and unruly aura. A portrait of a witch, I thought to myself as I approached.

She smiled, and her intentions were visible in the alluring pull of her smile. The kind of smile that made both men and women fall into a state of worship.

"You must be Wren," she said, her voice rich with a curling depth that wrapped you in her words like a gift.

"I've been expecting you," and then she unwrapped you with flirtatious intentions nestled in each syllable.

I froze—*I hadn't told her I was coming.* I hadn't told her my name.

" I-uh—how did you?"

Her eyes darted toward the painting in my arms. The corner of her mouth curved.

"You again," she murmured as she turned and walked inside, her long cloak sweeping across the floor. She didn't close the door behind her, so I followed.

I hesitated at the door. I was so close. Too close.

"Wh—what do you *mean* again?" I called into the seemingly empty house.

The smell of herbs and wax wafted into my nose. A subtle hint of patchouli, along with every incense I'd ever lit in college, slipped deeply into my sinuses, leaving them aching from the oversaturation.

"Set him down there," she gestured to a low table covered in deep velvet.

I delicately placed Ronan, the painting, on the table. Amelie leaned in close, her fingers covered in dark ink and tattoos hovering just above the frame. She hesitated to touch it, but I could tell she felt what I had felt.

She felt his heartbeat.

"How did you end up with him?" she asked, lighting a hand-rolled, papery joint that hung from her lips while she talked.

"An auction," I murmured, staring at it lying lifeless on the table, fully displayed.

"Do you have any idea what you've brought here?" Her voice cut through the air, and I couldn't tell if I had audacity or none.

"I know enough—I need help."

Her eyes snapped at mine. She gazed deeply into me. I could feel her picking apart my insecurities.

Help? She threw her head back and laughed, the smoke from her herb joint filling the air with the potent blend.

"Is that what you think I do?" She sauntered over to me, reaching her finger out, brushing it down my face, and tapping the tip of my nose like that of a child.

"This isn't his first time here." She smiled, "He didn't tell you that, though, did he?" She leaned in and whispered, "If he let you bring him here, you are already too far in."

She stood back, "How can I help?"

"Break the curse, set him free,"

Amelie blinked at me. Once. Twice.

Then she laughed—a deep, horrible cackle that didn't match the smooth, delicious voice of a seductive witch at all. It curled into my gut, striking me and nearly toppling me over.

"That is…. *Something.*" She wheezed, wiping a tear from her eye.

Her face met mine, and the wicked expression she had contorted her features into revealed that she realized at that moment that I wasn't joking.

She circled the table. "Ronan Arslane, you convinced this… bird. To set you free?" She was almost shouting at the painting, to which Ronan's face remained unmoved and unchanged from the day I'd hung it in my house.

"What tricks you must have learned, what games you must've played." She grabbed a few bottles of various concoctions and began pouring them over the top of the canvas.

"She wishes you *free*. Not vanquished, not exorcised, and not burned to a crisp like the last one."

"The last one?" My voice barely made a noise.

Ronan comes to visit me every so often. A new victim will claw at desperation to find a way to contain him, cleanse him." Amelie pointed to a charred mass on the other side of the room. "Send him back to hell.

My face turned cold and pale, and a bubbling sickness began to rise, but I forced it back down with a deep swallow.

I was a fool, a naïve, desperate fool. Of course, Ronan had lied. He not only knew about Amelie, but he had been here. He had survived this witch every time someone else discovered what I had.

"Last time, we almost went through with it, didn't we, *Ronan?*"

She puffed out a cloud of smoke and coughed, "Never has anyone asked for him to be *freed* from the Badlands."

"Th—The Badlands?" I questioned.

"My, he's told you so very little, and yet you want him free?" She smiled as she sprinkled a delicate powder in the shape of a star across the large painting.

"What did he offer you?" Amelie casually puffed on the herbal cigar, blowing giant clouds of its dense smoke into the little remaining air in the room.

"Endless riches? No, it couldn't be," she slowly talked around me, sizing me up and digging into my soul for answers I wouldn't give her.

"Power? Magic?" She was guessing.

"No," she whispered, "He didn't..." Her face grew serious, and her eyes widened.

"Did he promise to love you?" Her mouth creaked into a slow, daring smile.

"Oh, you poor girl, he *did.*" She moved in close to me. I could smell the faint scent of decay.

"He did no such thing. I could never love that monster," I snapped back, revealing too much in my outburst. I felt chilled and repulsed by the thought of loving Ronan.

She sighed deeply. "My, my, my... Ronan Arslane, The Cursed Knight. The one who thought he could defy Isolde Wyld and escape unscathed." She clicked her tongue. "This time, so close to freedom."

Her eyes flicked toward me as she licked her lips with an unmistakable kind of malice.

"You found a cursebreaker," she hummed low. Her voice descended into a deep, ungodly tone. Her eyes flashed a deep red. She was more than a woman in the woods—she was a monster.

Oh god, I'd made a terrible mistake. I shouldn't be here. Amelie was worse than Ronan, the way she took me apart piece by piece. The way she looked, it seemed like she'd eat me alive.

A familiar voice echoed behind me, "That's enough of your wild antics, Amelie." I turned sharply. Ronan's form peeled from the surface of the painting, his outline still shimmering with the magical paint that bound him to it.

My entire body tightened at the sight of him, an uncontrollable response. His eyes burned with fierce hatred, but it didn't seem like his gaze was directed at me. It appeared that, for once, there was something in the world that Ronan Arslane despised more than me. *Amelie.*

"Ronan, glad you could join us. I was about to indulge in my dessert before supper," Amelie released a monstrous cackle.

"It's been so long. My, you're looking dashing, awfully *human*."

"Not long enough, it seems." Ronan sighed.

What had I done?

They... *did* know each other.

And now, I was facing certain death from the phantom that had worn me thin over weeks of psychological torture and a witch who seemed very much like she was going to eat me.

"You won't touch her, Amelie," Ronan barked.

My internal panic grew silent. Was he... *protecting me?*

"Touch her? Oh no, it isn't *her* that I want. It's *you.*" She smiled and rubbed a thick red syrup over the empty painting.

"You've lingered too long, and these... run-ins are getting too frequent, too close for comfort. So, I offer you what you've always wanted." She paused, smearing the red substance across the empty canvas. It looked like blood. I didn't want to ask, but I thought it was congealed blood.

A spark of sickness began to return to me as I watched the congealed, clotted darkness spread across the painting I had once thought to be hauntingly beautiful.

"Freedom?" Ronan's jaw clenched. "At what cost, Amelie?"

"You must remain by my side, as my ward, under my rule and reign. To do with as I please."

"No," Ronan smiled—his response was instant.

Amelie's eyes narrowed, and her expression fell. She was no longer playful, her brows furrowed in confusion.

"Are you refusing this freedom, Ronan Arslane?" she questioned, choosing her words carefully toward him.

"Better the cage with her than freedom with you." His voice expressed a disgust I had never known it to possess.

Amelie's anger intensified, and her eyes twitched, struggling to contain the fury within her small frame. Her hair became wilder, and her eyes deepened to a crimson hue. She slammed her hands onto the table, which snapped and cracked beneath her force.

"I offer this only once," She seethed. "Ronan," she paused, her cadence paced and strong as if she'd calmed herself to make her point. "It doesn't sound much like she'll choose you."

Ronan stood, unflinching, forcing Amelie back with his glare. Her gaze lingered on me. "Time can't heal all wounds."

I stood, unable to respond, my words stolen from me.

I couldn't speak. My pulse pounded through my body. It was as if I had experienced the entire scene from across the room, like a fly on the wall. I watched myself experience the thrill of magic I didn't know existed.

Ronan chose a life trapped in a painting, in a place called the Badlands, but with me? In my house?

I snatched the painting from the table and used the velvet to wipe off whatever Amelie had tainted Ronan's canvas with. It splattered onto the floor and seared into the wood as if it had been ignited by fire.

I ran for my car, panting and out of breath. I looked back, and Amelie was watching me. I loaded Ronan's painting into the back seat, smacking it against every surface as I tried to fit it in quickly. I glanced toward Amelie's collapsing porch before getting into the driver's seat; she brought her finger to her neck and swiped it across, a warning. Her house blazed behind her, with smoke billowing ferociously into the sky.

Her threat felt like a scene from a horror movie, entirely unreal—impossible. There wasn't a need for such a warning. I wouldn't be coming back here—ever. When I was finally buckled in and reversing out of the long drive, the wheels of my sedan kicked up dust and stones, tossing them in every direction. I was at least a mile away when Amelie's whisper tickled my ears as if she were standing right behind me.

"Curses don't break for free, Wren."

Why did I take him with me? I could have left him there. Then it hit me... I thought I had taken Ronan to Amelie. But now I wasn't so sure.

Had he taken me?

♫ "River" – Bishop Briggs

CHAPTER 10

Unraveled

The storm had rolled in hours ago, and the house was battling against the fury of the wind. It felt unrelenting, as if we were trapped in the path of a tornado stuck in place.

I stared at my phone, my thumb hovering over Sam's name in my contacts. It had been too long since we last talked. He had sent me a few texts—

Sam: *You alive?*
Sam: *Did you die in that house?*
Sam: *Blink once if you're possessed*

but I left him on read, an offense punishable by death to Sam.

I wasn't exactly avoiding him. I was avoiding anything that might make me appear insane. I had to find a way to conceal the truth while also releasing everything I was holding inside.

I pressed the call button.

"Holy shit, she lives." Sam's voice was full of mock horror. "I was a day away from calling the police, or worse—your mom."

"Truly terrifying threats," I muttered, pulling my blanket tighter around me. The flicker of emergency candles cast my shadow grotesquely and hauntingly against the tall living room walls.

"I just—Meh, fuck it—I've been throwing myself into distractions, work. I have a new client, and it's keeping me busy."

"The client is keeping you busy, or is someone else?"

My entire body clenched at Sam's intuition.

"What? No. No way, I'm not ready to date yet."

"Oh my god, there's a guy," Sam said, stripping me of any cover. "Wren. The hell? You're seeing someone, and you didn't tell me? Betrayal."

"There's no *guy*."

"Then it's a woman because your voice is all low and fluffy like you're in love."

I scoffed, "I didn't call to talk about me. What's going on with you?" I rubbed my temples and closed one eye.

"My life is exactly the same as it was when you left. I put it on pause, like a game of Mario Kart," he snickered. "Because I only do my best living when you are in the same city as me."

I laughed, "God, you're the worst."

"And you are living alone in an old haunted house in the middle of nowhere. You can't just talk to the walls. You'll go crazy," he sighed. "So?"

"I have *one* friend, actually."

"Oh?" Sam's voice sounded interested.

"She met a guy, and he's an arrogant, insufferable asshole."

"Your friend has a type—keep going."

I exhaled, forcing my voice to find its grounding. "She hates him. But she also can't seem to get rid of him."

Silence.

Then, Sam inhaled sharply.

"Wren. Is this a 'you need me to help bury a body' call?

I snorted. "No."

"Because we really shouldn't talk about this on the phone," Sam laughed. I could hear his smile through the phone. He was enjoying this as much as I was.

"Your friend might be dating a serial ki—"

I interrupted whatever Sam was going to say next.

"He's just..." I struggled to find the words, "He gets under her skin. He's always there, pushing, provoking, and making her feel things she doesn't want to."

Another long pause.

Then, Sam let out a low whistle. "Hot."

I blinked. "What?"

"I mean, is he hot?"

"What does that have to do with *anything*?"

"Everything, Wren, everything. Ugly men are dangerous. Hot men are just a bad decision you live to regret."

"This is not how I saw this going," I laughed, slurping wine from my glass while I laughed off Sam's jokes.

"There's an acceptable amount of crazy we're willing to put up with if an achingly delicious man delivers it," he said. I could hear him closing cabinets in his kitchen.

I groaned and covered my head with my blanket.

Sam was quiet for a moment. Then, in a rare serious tone, he said, "Does she feel safe? Your friend?"

The question hit like an arrow directly into my heart.

"If she's hesitating, she already has her answer," Sam added amidst the chaos of my thoughts.

I thought of Ronan's hands around my throat.

Of his voice, whispering threats in the dark.

His body pressed against me, his mouth against my skin without my consent.

And worst of all—the way I wanted him anyway.

" I-I don't know," I admitted, whispering.

Sam exhaled, "Then she should run."

There was something to be said about Sam when he was serious. His voice lost its rainbow aura and sank deep into the darkest night. If Sam told you to run, you ran. But I wasn't running.

Sam told me to *run,* and I was ignoring him on purpose.

And that's what scared me most of all.

***

The fire crackled softly from across the room. I had finally managed to get it lit. The storm dropped droplets of rain onto the coals, causing my flame to fizzle out each time it ignited.

But finally, the fire prevailed.

Thunder roared outside, whipping the nearby trees into a frantic display. The wind howled against the old windows, and for a moment, I felt small; the house felt larger than ever.

Ronan had chosen me. *Me.* Not freedom, not escape.

He stayed. For me. With me.

It had felt romantic at first—grand, sweeping, and wildly insane—a gesture straight from the pages of a romance novel. But as I sank into the blankets in my bed, watching the fire roar, it felt... manipulative.

Sam's words echoed in the depths of my mind, over and over, like a warning I wanted to ignore.

Was this love?

Could you love the insinuation of a person as a revenant? Could a phantom steal your heart *and* take your breath away without killing you? Was it reckless and unhinged to be madly in love with a ghost? And was something like this even sustainable, or was I categorically insane and a breath away from being committed?

The floorboards creaked at my doorway. I didn't need to turn to know it was him. I could feel his presence filling the air around me, sending an electrifying current through every part of my body.

"Say something," I whispered, my voice trembling. "Don't just stand there. It gives me the creeps, Ronan," I said firmly, confidently.

"I'm here," Ronan whispered in a low, scratchy growl. There was something visceral about his response. "Isn't that enough?"

I turned my head toward the darkness of his shape, like something from a fever dream. The fire illuminated all the right parts of him, making him appear more human, more real than I'd ever seen him before. It highlighted the subtle tension in his jaw, the slow sweeping muscles that lined his neck, and the peaks of strong, protruding clavicles under his button-down shirt.

It was as if, with each passing day, he connected more deeply to the human in me and adapted. I wanted to look away, to tear my attention off him, but I couldn't. This wasn't a ghost. It was a man, and any hesitation I had about his phantom form melted away, slipping out of my grasp.

I felt trapped, his eyes devouring me with each slow breath I released, and nothing was holding me back. Nothing was clouding my judgment.

"I don't know if it is," I said honestly while my heart thudded wildly. I lowered my guard, revealing my vulnerability. "You've taken away every choice I have left, Ronan. What do you expect me to do?" I asked, wanting to know... what was the answer.

Did he want me to be a prisoner or a willing participant?

"You still have a choice," he said, stepping closer. I pushed myself toward the edge of the bed, sitting up straight and facing him now.

"Walk away. I'll tell you how." His eyes conveyed something his words didn't. He stood in front of me, looking down, while I looked up over his body, the ripples of it bending light to create it.

He reached out, and his timid, soft fingers brushed against my cheek, tightening everything inside me. His touch was alive, and his fingers had a warmth I hadn't known a ghost could have.

I should have pulled myself away. I should scream at him to get out. I should have defied him, pushed harder against his undeniable pull.

I should have done anything but the soft whimper that escaped my mouth as I leaned into his touch. His thumb traced the curve of my jaw, and I watched him as if he were still dangerous, as if he could strike and end me at any moment.

A hesitant whisper let out what I was thinking. "I still hate you." I was barely able to breathe while his hands touched me. His thumb brushed over my lips, and I could feel him thinking about where he wanted them.

"Good." A smile crossed his lips.

And then I was kissing him.

It wasn't tentative. There was no hesitation in him. He wasn't curious or wondering. This kiss was a response, an answer to all that I'd asked myself, and certainty vibrated through my entire body as I surrendered to the force that propelled us so violently toward one another.

His arms wrapped around me, and I could feel their strength. They held me as if I were something both breakable and wild at once. His kiss deepened, and I felt everything and nothing. The slightest movement from him flared my senses. I felt his hands pressed against my skin. It felt exactly how I'd imagined it and so much more.

The dreams, the visions, the hauntings locked in a moment that wasn't happening—all of it felt exactly like how I felt in Ronan's arms.

It felt like silk being teased gently over me, or like heavy, warm velvet pulled across my skin. He grew bolder with each second. His touch became more chaotic, as if he wanted to be everywhere at once. He couldn't find a single place to land. He had to flutter past all of me, teasing and awakening them all at once.

I sank deeply into the bed. It felt as if I had reached the bottom of the room while his mouth pressed delicate kisses across my body, teasing his tongue in waves over me.

He buried his face deep between my legs and forced my hands into the shadows of his hair. I grasped and gripped him while he feasted on me like a banquet he had longed to consume for centuries.

I felt each tempered press and each delightful swirl of his tongue passing over me in a slow and steady rhythm. I curled my body into an arch, and my legs began to tremor with a rising pleasure, and within seconds, the darkness of his shape was under me. I was straddled delicately over him. His expression was blank but filled with a comforting pleasure.

He was *enjoying* himself.

His hands gripped my waist. He adapted to a slow rhythm, pressing forward and pulling back, revealing what would happen next if I desired it.

I had all the choices.

I could stop.

I could climb out of this bed and wish Ronan gone.

He'd leave. I knew he would.

Or...

I whispered, "Are you sure?" into his ear, my voice barely audible.

"Never more," he panted back as I slid down onto him, and we both instantly let out a cry for a God neither believed in.

Time stood still as we paused, allowing a moment to catch our breath. Seconds passed, and as we grew accustomed to the feeling of being together, it transformed into a warming heat.

Each subtle breath he took, whether real or theatrical, tantalized me. I felt every inch of him grow harder and press further until I begged for him.

He'd said I'd beg.

He knew all along that we'd end up in this moment, as if he had planned it or seen it using whatever curse magic he possessed.

He wasn't wrong. I begged, and Ronan lifted me and pressed me down onto him, over and over, each time going deeper and further than the time before, taking with him my breath, my sanity.

I broke open and poured onto him over and over again, calling out his name like I'd free him from his curse and drench him in my humanity.

I offered myself as a sacrifice.

Ronan Arslane left me broken for any other man or phantom for all eternity.

All at once, he became my God. He was the church to which I would kneel and worship. He embodied all the colors and the light of the purest heart, but he was also my captor and King—the darkest shadow of the night. He was the specter you scurried away from and the shapes you didn't see when you thought you had.

He was the dark you should fear, but only because he'd make you beg for more of him.

And I would *never* let him go.

♫ "Dangerous Woman" – Ariana Grande

CHAPTER 11

Queen

The air smelled faintly of smoke and storm-drenched morning air, mingled with something else: Ronan. I pressed my fingers to my lips, expecting them to burn from the memory of his engulfing kiss.

I hated how much I wanted him again.

The visions were uncontrollable and would strike unexpectedly, but if I controlled my breathing, targeted my thoughts, and focused on something obscure like baseball or my mother's lasagna recipe, I could fight off the visions.

I could fight against being pulled back into my memory, where Ronan did unholy things to my b—

Suddenly, I wasn't in the kitchen anymore; I was in bed...

I gasped, and my fingers clenched around the outer edge of the counter.

No. No. Not again.

The phantom sensation washed over me in relentless waves. His lips on my neck, his hands gripping my waist. The way he had whispered my name in the calm moments of our fury.

I squeezed my eyes shut. I wasn't there. I was in my kitchen, making coffee. I sighed and leaned heavily against the countertop, trying desperately to catch my breath.

This was exhausting.

But suddenly, a rough moan escaped my throat as I was dragged back under again, his mouth hot and insistent. The sound of my own call to him. The way he had—

The coffee maker's drip-stop alarm pierced the air.

I lurched back, and my mug shattered against the floor, ceramic glass bursting out in every direction.

This had to stop. I needed to get out of this house. Out of his reach. Out of whatever was dragging me into a reality that may soon be inescapable.

There is a whole world outside of Ronan Arslane.

I hated him.

I hated how he made me feel like he was using the knowledge I hadn't given him to press the right buttons and say the right words. He was an ethereal presence that wielded my greatest fears and desires against me. He was manipulative, and I was merely a pawn in this game he played to alleviate his incessant centuries of boredom.

But *God...* I felt so alive. Every synapse in my brain was firing. Every tingle of my skin was a recognition of my humanity. I hated how he had taken up so much space in my life without asking... and now I had to find a way to live with or around him.

My phone buzzed. I reached for it.

Mr. Ashford's name lit up on the screen—a *distraction*.

"Miss Rivers," he said when I answered, his voice hesitant and uncertain. If I hadn't met him face to face, I would agree that his voice didn't reflect his stature. He was a towering man with Southern charm. This was something I'd ignored at the time but remembered upon hearing the subtle twang in how he'd said my name.

"I trust you're well?" Even the way he asked about my day was charming.

"Mr. Ashford," I said, straightening my posture slightly, catching my breath, and tucking my hair behind my ear. "Good morning,"

I pushed aside the memories of last night, focusing on a stain on the counter.

"Miss Rivers, I hope this isn't too forward, but..." he paused. "I'm rather taken by you, and I was wondering if perhaps you'd let me take you to dinner?" The request shocked me. I hadn't expected this, not even slightly.

"Oh, my," I was blushing. The red seared my cheeks. "That sounds lovely—tonight?"

"Seven O'clock, I'll see you then," he replied, far more confident than he had been when introducing himself. The call ended, and I stared at the screen for a moment, processing the interaction.

"Who was that?"

Ronan's voice came from the doorway, low and cold.

His eyes burned with an intensity I rarely saw in him—in fact, I had only seen it once when I cursed him with Isolde's name, and he nearly strangled me. He looked like a predator, tearing apart his prey.

"No one," I said, "It's dinner with a—"

"Another man?" His words cut through my bullshit.

I rolled my eyes, forcing a casualness I didn't feel. "It's a business contact, Ronan."

Ronan's jaw clenched at the attitude I'd laced my response with.

His fists tightened, and his eyes narrowed on me. I braced myself, knowing what was coming next, but instead, I was hit with a curveball.

"You belong to me."

My eyes widened, "Excuse me?" My pulse quickened.

"You belong to me, Wren. No other man will touch you." His voice deepened and turned into a whisper. His possessiveness seeped into each low syllable that tumbled from his lips without care.

"I don't *belong* to anyone," I snapped. "And you don't get to tell me who I can and can't see."

He moved quickly, closing the distance between us in less than a heartbeat. I had prepared for it, so when he slammed against me, gripping firmly at my throat, I had expected this. His other hand locked my wrists above my head. I was helpless. He sent a shock of energy through me.

"I chose you," he said, his voice trembling with a rage laced with fear.

"Let me go," I commanded.

For a moment, I thought he wouldn't. He gripped my throat firmly, tightening his hold as my vision began to blur and my muscles started to give out. He released his grip, and I doubled over, gasping for air.

"You can't do that," I said, my voice quieter. "You can't keep *me* in a cage just because *you're in one.*"

"I would never, Little Bird." he said softly, a stark change from the voice threatening my life.

"But I will not share, and do not underestimate the lengths I might—"

"Do not finish your sentence, Ronan Arslane." I stared deeply into his wildly alive eyes. He was nearly entirely human now. The only evidence of his former specter self was that when he moved quickly, his edges blurred as if blended into reality with a brush. You'd never notice it if you weren't looking for it.

"I see I am still just a pawn, Ronan," I smiled at him with deep hate. "We'll finish this later. I have dinner to get ready for." I turned my smile into a scowl and stormed off toward my bedroom.

***

The restaurant was located on a busy street downtown, near the place where I bought Ronan, which made me chuckle slightly. It featured low, intimate lighting and crisp white tablecloths, enhancing the significance of the meal.

Mr. Ashford stood as I entered, offering a warm, disarming smile that instantly put my anxiety at ease. He was comfortable.

He appeared normal, steady—nothing like the wreck of a specter I'd left back at the house.

"You look stunning, Miss Rivers," He said, pulling out my chair. "Thank you for joining me on such short notice."

"It's nice to get out," I said, settling into the chair. "It seems like all I do is talk to ghosts these days," I teased. No one would ever realize the truth in it.

While I was getting ready, the house was filled with suffocating tension. Ronan had thrown dishes around and sent my makeup bag tumbling down the stairs. I used remnants from the shattered containers to pull myself together, but inside, I felt as broken as they now were, too.

I wouldn't let it interfere with experiencing a moment of normalcy. I choked it down and buried it under a layer of wine Mr. Ashford had presumed I'd enjoy. With each sip, I forced myself not to wonder about the terrible scene I'd walk back into after the ramifications of defying my harrowing haunt of a roommate.

The waiter arrived, and Mr. Ashford ordered a second bottle of wine as we slipped effortlessly into conversation. He was undoubtedly charming in all the right ways, and it felt natural to discuss the complexities of life with him. The way his eyes sparkled with excitement at every word you spoke made you feel like the most important person in the room. Perhaps even that you were the only person alive.

For the first time in what felt like years, I relaxed; my shoulders dropped slightly, and I let the weight of everything I held fall from them. The wine sipped easily, and my cheeks flushed with the excitement of a buzz.

"I've been meaning to ask," he said after a while, his voice lowering to a discreet whisper. "How are you finding life here? It must be... lonely, living alone, your friends hundreds of miles from you?"

"It's peaceful, actually." The word rang hollow even in my own ears. I knew it was a lie, and I believed he did too.

He nodded thoughtfully, his eyes attentive. "Ah, peace. Something I aspire to find," he paused and swirled his wine. "Life does have a way of surprising us. It always finds a way to bring us what we need. Bring us to the people we need."

I smiled, though something about his words struck deeper.

"Mr. Ashford, do I hear the words of an optimist, or are my ears deceiving me?" I teased.

"Ah, you caught me, Miss Rivers. That, I am. That... I am," He sighed, "But I like to think of it as hopeful."

I scoffed lightly, *hope*. Ronan's biggest fear. No wonder he was so afraid of Mr. Ashford. He had found a nemesis.

"I'll be honest, Miss Rivers," he stopped and smiled at a passing waiter. "I can't wait," his grin, surprisingly, pulled even wider on his handsome face. "I can't wait to find the love that turns my world on its axis. The kind that brings me to my knees and changes everything."

"Not everyone finds that." As the phrase fluttered from my lips, I realized I was the table's resident pessimist.

"I think they do," He said gently, "But only if they're open to it."

For a brief moment, I watched the words flow from his mouth, the way his lips creased with the close of each syllable, and I wandered deeply into the idea of what it would be like to fall in love with someone like Mr. Ashford.

This was the wine's perspective, and certainly not mine—because mine would still be fixated on the darkened shadow of a man who wanted to both take and give me life simultaneously.

But this—this was a man who saw love as a gift, not a weapon. A man who would never make me feel like I had to fight for every breath, but rather that I was worthy of the air that filled my lungs and so much *more*.

He asked about my work, interests, and what attracted me to this town. He was careful, kind, and always listened more than he spoke. However, there was something deeper beneath his kindness—concern, perhaps? He never expressed it directly, but it was there... in his eyes.

"You seem... restless," he said, his brown furrowing slightly. He looked disappointed. "Like you're caught between places."

The observation stopped me, but I played in, "What do you mean?"

He smiled, but there was something wistful in it. "It's just a feeling. You remind me of someone standing at the edge of a decision." He shifted, "You look ready to jump, but not sure who will catch you when you do."

For a second, I thought he *knew.* Not the details, but the parts of my life I hadn't shared. He saw that I was teetering on the crack between two worlds.

"Those are some heavy observations for just dinner, Mr. Ashford," I rubbed my finger along the outer edge of the now-empty wine glass.

"Is there something you want to ask me?" I raised my eyebrow just as the waiter came by and poured my glass significantly fuller than before.

Was I so shattered that it was easy to see, or was he something else I needed to be concerned about?

Mr. Ashford observed me for a moment, his fingers drumming against the stem of his glass. He exhaled as if weighing the decision to press forward or retreat. Then, with a measured smile, he leaned back in his chair, taking the hint.

"No, Miss Rivers, no questions. Just an observation." He swirled the wine in his glass, "I've learned something in my line of work—people carry the weight of their choices long before they realize they've already made them." His eyes met mine, searching. "You just look like someone who's already jumped. You're just waiting to see where you land."

Tension coiled in my stomach. I had wanted him to back off, but now that he had, I almost hated having let him. It was a skill I had perfected—pulling away the second someone got too close.

I laughed softly, "You should have been a poet, Mr. Ashford."

"Ah, I wouldn't dare. I very rarely find the right words for the moment; this just so happens to be one of those rare occasions." He sipped his wine, his gaze lingering on me long enough to make me wonder what he thought he understood about me.

I mirrored his movement, taking a slow sip of my own. "Rare, indeed."

***

The evening concluded quietly, with Mr. Ashford insisting on driving me home. The conversation lingered, having been so engaging and complex, with so much to relive. Yet one sentence replayed like a song stuck in my head.

"The kind of love that brings me to my knees and changes everything."

When we arrived at the house, I hesitated in the car, unwilling to step back into the shadows of what was raging inside. Mr. Ashford must have sensed it.

"If you ever need anything—anything at all—don't hesitate to call," he said, his hand resting briefly on mine. It felt steady and warm, solid, causing a natural release of tension.

"Thank you," I said, giving the handsome man a half-smile of genuine affection. "Do reconsider giving poetry a try. Your gift shouldn't go wasted." I winked as I closed the door and exited the car.

I watched his taillights dwindle into tiny glowing red baubles of a faded memory. I turned toward the house and took a deep breath, preparing to walk back into a trap I'd set myself.

I set my keys and bag down at the door, and their jingle landing in the clay bowl echoed through the house. It rang out as if it were empty, making me wonder if Ronan had decided to leave. Had all it taken was a show of force, a quiet I will not be controlled, to make him disappear?

I reached down and slipped off my heels. Their clatter was sharp against the wood. It was cold. But a breath of warmth made me realize I wasn't alone.

"You're late," Ronan's voice growled from under the shadows.

I nearly lurched at the surprising sound. It startled me with its closeness, but the wine I'd indulged in had sedated me quite a bit. He'd have to try harder to scare me now.

"I didn't know I was on a curfew," my pulse quickened at my response. Purposefully rebellious, intentionally coy, and definitely defiant.

Ronan stepped into the dim light. He'd let the fire die, and the house was filled instead with his cold jealousy. I could see my breath unfurling from my mouth as I exhaled.

"You were with him for a long time."

"Don't start," I said, brushing past him. He could have stopped me. He could have pinned me against the wall and reminded me of what he was capable of, but he didn't.

"It was just dinner." I kept my voice light, but I was inching toward daring him to deny me a fundamental right.

"Just *dinner*." He repeated, his voice calm.

"I can smell the wine on your skin. You've been drinking."

"Yes," I snapped back. "Not that it's any of your business."

I knew I was provoking him; I wanted to. I wanted to claw at him, to dig under his skin like he did to me. It was like playing with fire—I wanted to get burned.

Because I deserved this darkness.

I deserved this pain.

I deserved *him.*

I let out a small laugh, breathless, a little reckless.

I *didn't* deserve a perfect Mr. Ashford, *no.*

I deserved the evil of Ronan Arslane.

And then, faster than I could register, *he had me.*

His hand curled around my wrist—firm but not painful. It felt like a protective grasp, with a hesitation in his touch, as if he were stopping me from burning myself.

"You deserve to be treated like a Queen." He murmured.

I froze—*Had he heard my thoughts? Could he tell what I was thinking?*

"Then show me." My breath caught at his words, but I issued the demand regardless. Not a taunt but an invitation. A plea.

I saw something different flash in his eyes—not rage or possession, as he'd try to make me believe with this dance. It was hunger, but not the kind that sought to consume; rather, it was the kind that wanted to worship.

His grip tightened for just a second—his body pulling closer, his breath tickling the edges of my skin. His mask was slipping. I felt it. His fingers twitched, an erratic movement for him; he was never this hesitant.

My rosy, wine-stained lips parted, needing to let out more air as my breath built up. His eyes were glued to me, to my mouth. But the moment snapped, and the chill of the room rushed between us.

He released and stepped away, finally saying, "I'll show you." He whispered, "You'll see."

But the damage was already done.

I'd felt it.

I felt him want to surrender.

And now, I knew—no matter how much he fought it—I was winning.

♫ "Bad Intentions" – Niykee Heaton

CHAPTER 12

Cursebreaker

Ronan broke open in front of me. His words flowed from him like a soliloquy—a poem of pain and a song of sorrow. Centuries of pain, of loss… a circumstance so vast that I couldn't wrap my mind around how a soul could survive such atrocities.

I knew he was bitter. I had seen his violence from the moment we met. I felt it coil beneath him and wrap around his heart, waiting for a release.

'The Badlands," he said, his voice low and haunted. "It's a place made up of your own mind's design. I've heard of phantoms and the cursed living wondrous lives in the vast realm where we're free to wander to our heart's desires." Ronan shook his head.

"They're lies, but they're pleasant." His gaze drifted off as if he were reentering the desolate land he spoke of so carefully.

"The Badlands is what you make of it. For many, it's a darkened land of emptiness—a hopeless land, barren and devoid of color and light. The sky is forever layered under a shroud of ambient darkness." His eyes met mine. His words felt like poetry because of how tragic they were, but I sensed the pain behind them and recognized them as Ronan's truth.

"Many wander until they become the haunting shadows of the forests and live silently among the trees, their bodies turned to swaying apparitions paralyzed in their loneliness." He sighed and leaned back.

I'd never seen him so vulnerable before.

"The Badlands taunts you into submission, begging you to crack and crumble under its demands. Some wander, searching, waiting... for their cursebreaker." He tilted his head as if he were painting a picture not unlike the one he had been imprisoned in.

"Their *cursebreaker?*" I whispered.

"Curses..." He paused to plan his explanation. "Curses can sometimes choose their end. If not by their maker, not by blood— by the breaker." Ronan sang it like it was a song.

"Chosen by my curse, you are mine." He looked shamefully toward the ground.

"Is that why—" I remembered when he was still in his shadow form; he'd called out that I was his. He meant that I was his cursebreaker.

"Many never find theirs. They walk the Badlands among the madness of their insanity, and emptiness consumes them." He took a deep breath and shifted his stance.

"I survived centuries. Alone. Every day, I expected to meet that end and become one of the frozen shadows. But the Badlands, *Isolde*, never let me go."

He hesitated before he said her name, "Isolde had made a deal with the devil himself, *The Keeper*, who sits quietly brooding among the Badland's fiercest monsters, ruling over them like minions of darkness." He reached over toward me and brushed his hands over the tear that unknowingly slid down my cheek

"Isolde didn't just curse me, but she exiled me to a place where hope is punishable with simply more empty, never-ending *life.*"

Hearing the full extent of his truth shattered my heart as if it could be broken any more than it had been before. The Badlands—the suffering, the way Isolde had confined him in a place worse than death, worse than the most vicious version of Hell you could imagine. It wasn't just cruelty. It was a crucible.

It was beyond me how Ronan still had any humanity left in his soul. It spoke to how truly miraculous a being he really was. How great must one be for this world to withstand the weight of such an ending?

"This canvas... a window into a world I could never be a part of. A tease, a reminder of all the curse had taken from me." He paused, looking at the empty frame still secured to the wall.

"I thought Isolde to have mercy, but this canvas. It wasn't merciful, no." His voice grew more tattered with each word, his edges fraying, coming undone with each advancing thought.

"I'd been able to step through, *occasionally.* And I haunted those women and men the same. I'd tear their sanity apart, piece by piece. Each time, using them to find my way back to Amelie, to see if she would relinquish me from my curse." He paused and looked at me as if he were waiting for something. "Amelie has never offered me freedom."

"Men? Women? Are they—"

"Gone—Amelie would toss me back out into the world after they'd begged her for salvation, and she consumed them."

I gasped. I had been so close to her. She could have—

"She would have tried and failed." He read my mind.

He shook his head and stepped toward the window. "I don't know how or why, Little Bird." The way he whispered my little nickname brought a slight smile to his voice.

"But Amelie feared you—it's how I knew you were *more*."

He stood by the fireplace, his hands pressed against the ornate mantel as if he could brace himself against the onslaught of memories. His knuckles were white, bearing the pressure of his weight. The tendons of his forearms bulged, tension woven throughout every inch of his tightening body.

His chest rose and fell with uneven breaths, and I realized that this was the first time he had ever shared this part of the life he'd experienced.

"Wren." He was raw, his voice cracked.

"Say something."

I had no words. I had nothing to console him. Nothing I could offer would be enough to undo the torture. I was just Wren Rivers, a photographer from a city who ran away from a slightly cracked heart and humiliation.

I wasn't a queen or a cursebreaker. I wasn't worth the breath it took to tell my story. I stood in the shadow of something holy, something magical. Yet, he was mine.

I did the only thing I could think of.

I closed the distance and pressed my hands against his. He flinched under my touch, yet he didn't pull away. Slowly, he turned, his gaze searching mine, and in it, I saw everything.

"Share it," I whispered. My fingers interlaced with his.

"Share it with me," I begged him.

"*Wren*—No." Ronan lowered his gaze to the ground, his eye winced.

I rose onto my toes, pressing my lips against him, pulling his pain into myself while bearing the ache in my heart as well.

He released what he had held back, and I felt it hit me—the pressure, the all-consuming blackness of a soul caught in a mediocre existence. It nearly knocked me back, and my knees began to buckle under its weight.

It twisted inside me, contorting my heart, wrenching it down and bursting it into millions of shattered, unmendable pieces. I felt what he'd felt and instantly recognized the reason for everything.

We leaned into one another, sharing the pain together, two souls intertwined forever. Our connection was different from before. It was not a battle or a clash of defiance and hate. This was a surrender, a mutual right to relinquish what ailed us both.

His fingers traced up my arms and across my collarbone reverently, as if he were searching for a way to hold my heart together while it felt his history claw into it, applying pressure to prevent it from shattering completely.

My hands slipped into his hair, pulling him closer. I wrapped my body around him as we floated in the air. It was an ethereal moment that I knew would last forever for both of us.

He let out a groan as I pressed against him fully, his hands gripping desperately on my hips. But he didn't rush. Every moment was slow, intentional. He wanted to force out the memories of the Badlands that overwhelmed him and replace them with the curves of my body, the warmth our skin created when it was pressed against one another. He buried his face in my neck and exhaled shakily.

"You are the first thing I've truly wanted in five hundred years." His lips found my shoulder as the words fluttered over my skin. "And I'm scared that I won't get to keep you."

"I'm here," I paused. "Isn't that enough?" I rang his words back to him. We reached the bed, and he hesitated. His hand curled around my wrist, uncertain. "Are you sure?"

"Never more," I whispered, and I gripped him harder between my legs, entangling him with me as we crashed down. There was nothing that could take this moment from us. We would rewrite him and carve over every memory of Isolde until no space was left for her inside him.

This world was just made for us.

He released any reservations, and the slow, deliberate press of him inside me ignited a heat that branded me as his forever. The way his mouth traced along my body, clearing a path down my throat, with his teeth gently scraping against my skin, served as a reminder that behind his passion lay a monster that could tear into me unprovoked.

His hands caressed me carefully, as if touching something sacred. I invited him to shatter me and take me into the darkness where he had lived for so long, to bury me deep in despair. But he graciously nibbled, delicately unraveling me in a way that brought his name to my lips in holy praise.

He centered himself, bracing against my body, and leaned in with a powerful force that knew no boundaries, pulling and pushing my hips so that I gripped around him like two perfect pieces meant for one another.

I grasped and clawed to hold onto him, pulling him in closer, not letting him fade away but keeping him tethered to me. For a moment, a fleeting, delicate moment, I thought that maybe, just maybe, I could be enough to make him feel fully alive again.

I didn't know how to break a curse, but I would give it everything I had, even if it killed me.

🎵 "Rivers and Roads" – The Head And The Heart

CHAPTER 13

Birthday

His dark lashes fanned over his cheekbones, and for a moment, he resembled any other man. No curses or banishments to shadowed worlds. Not centuries trapped in a desolate painting. His hand remained wrapped around mine, fingers woven together as if they were meant to be affixed, permanent.

"Stay," I whispered, not knowing if I meant in bed, in my life, or both.

His eyes flicked open—softened by the euphoria of the night before. "Always," he whispered, but a lingering shadow stood behind it, as if he couldn't fully agree to the promise.

I wanted to believe him, to trust that we had all the time in the world. But then the doorbell rang, and the reality of life came crashing into this sentimental moment I wished to remember for eternity.

Ronan stiffened beside me, his gaze sharpening, "Expecting someone?"

"No," I reached for my robe and tightened it around my body

"But shouldn't we answer when trouble knocks?" I smiled.

I padded to the door and opened it, blinded by the sudden burst of light. I'd almost forgotten that sunlight existed. As soon as my eyes focused, Ivy stood there, clutching a glittery gift bag, her face breaking into a wide grin. Beside her, Sam held a mismatched bouquet of wildflowers and wore his trademark mischievous expression.

"Surprise!" Ivy flung her arms around me, nearly knocking me back. "Happy birthday, Wren!"

My Birthday?

I had completely forgotten. Time had slipped away from me lately. Each day blended into the next, and I found myself entrapped in conversations with Ronan—lost in his stories of forgotten worlds.

We were constantly wandering in our connection, and during the days and nights, we discovered each other in a tangled mess of love and chaos. I had missed entire days enveloped by him and entwined with him in bed.

In the shower.

On the kitchen countertops.

Every floor, every wall...

The clawfoot tub that had once been a place I'd vowed to end him...

I shook the image of that moment out of my head.

"Wh—what are you guys doing here?" I asked, excited and nervous, glancing between them.

"We had nothing better to do, so we drove hundreds of miles to see you, obviously," Sam said, brushing past me and pushing his way into the house.

"You didn't think you could hide from us forever, did you?" He looked around at the high ceilings and the ornate moldings.

"What are you hiding in here?" he asked, pushing his glasses up the bridge of his nose. I pulled my robe tighter over my body. I was grossly underdressed.

Ivy followed him inside and carefully closed the door. Her eyes immediately scanned the space with curiosity, creating a knot in my stomach. I wouldn't be able to explain Ronan to Ivy. She knew so much but was also a force and would see through anything I tried to concoct.

She paused in the entryway, her gaze fixed on Ronan, who now stood carefully by the fireplace with his arms crossed. Her eyes widened, recognition dawning on her immediately.

"Ronan... Arslane?" her voice cracked with concern.

Sam snickered, glancing between us. "So, that's what you're hiding," He grinned slyly.

My cheeks blushed. This was chaos. This was the worst possible—

"Wait, what is happening right now," he said, his hands pointing back and forth between us flamboyantly. He must have seen the flush of my cheeks.

"Who is Mr. Tall-Dark-and-Broody over here? And why don't I know his name?" Sam pushed past Ivy and extended his hand toward Ronan.

I lost my words, and all I could find was a lie, "Oh, silly me, this is Ronan. He's... visiting?"

Ronan reached out and casually shook Sam's hand firmly. Sam's eyebrows raised as he turned and winked at me.

I should have been more assertive. He's staying here. Tell them he's staying here.

"He's *staying*—"

Ivy's eyes were glued to Ronan. She *knew.* She'd helped me discover Ronan's heritage. She interrupted me, "But, you're a painting." She didn't ask. She was telling him.

"Oh, Ivy, he is a vision, isn't he?" Sam raised an eyebrow. "A perfect painting!" Sam wandered toward the kitchen. "Where's the coffee, Wren? I need a caffeine drip stat."

His voice faded into a murmur before a clatter of cups and spoons echoed from the kitchen.

"It's complicated, Ivy," I begged her not to expose Ronan.

Not yet. Don't tell her yet—

"You must be a relative of the Ronan in the painting I studied," Ivy glanced deeply into my eyes. I let out a deep sigh.

"Yes, exactly. It was a portrait of an ancestor," Ronan nodded and smiled at Ivy.

Ivy eyed him, "Was?"

***

Dinner felt uncomfortable. The tension was palpable. Ronan remained perfectly composed, responding to questions with just enough ambiguity to remain convincing.

Sam, bless his heart. He was oblivious and filled the space with stories from back home, his easy humor keeping things from spiraling.

But Ivy watched Ronan like a hawk.

She waited for the perfect moment, and I found myself cornered while cleaning in the kitchen. Sam kept Ronan occupied while Ivy dug her intuitive little claws into me for the truth.

"That's him. The real Ronan Arslane. Not some distant relative."

I sighed, pressing my palms on the counter. "It's... complicated."

"Try me," She pushed her hands onto her hips and drilled her stare into me.

I couldn't hide it anymore.

"Did that man, out there... step out of a 500-year-old painting?" Her question was furiously direct.

I hesitated and slowly nodded.

Her face lit up, not with fear, but with wonder.

"Why wouldn't you tell me?"

"I didn't know how to say it. It sounds insane. I sound insane." I replied, catching my breath from the adrenaline of my deceit.

Ivy rested a hand on my shoulder. "Wren, please don't do stuff like this alone. I am always here, insane or not."

A tear formed in the corner of my eye. I wasn't alone. I didn't have to bear this weight by myself. It was a freeing moment—one I needed and hadn't realized. Ivy's eyes welled with the same tears, and she flung her arms around me. She squeezed, and the pressure felt firm and grounding.

"We have to... be careful. Curses don't *break* without a price." Her eyes darted, "But, um, for research purposes... I need to know... how is phantom fucking?" She used her hands to indicate what naughty thing she meant. "Specter sex? I mean, what are we calling it?"

"He's human now," I said, smiling.

Ivy's eyes flinched slightly with concern. She knew, just as I did, that he wasn't human. Not yet.

✳✳✳

Sam suggested a trip into town. I almost said no—the idea of leaving Ronan behind felt like tearing myself in half. I hadn't spent much time away from him, but the thought of him being alone for even a second tore me apart.

He had spent so many years alone, and I couldn't— but Ivy's pleading eyes finally convinced me. Ronan was too willing to let me go before I scampered out the door. I found myself enveloped in his massive arms. His touch reminded me of everything waiting for me when I came home.

"I won't be long," I brushed my lips over his neck, and he growled at the tease. "Take your time. I want you to *miss me*." He smiled.

I closed the door, taking one last look at the house. I smiled faintly at Ivy and Sam. "So..." My eyes darted between them. "What's the plan?"

"Are you serious?" Sam's eyes squinted in disgust. "Coffee. Always coffee first, Wren." He shook his head.

"Who are you even anymore?"

Ivy let out a cackle as we pulled away from the house. I glanced back once and allowed myself only a fleeting moment of regret for leaving Ronan.

✳✳✳

The café was filled with the scent of richly roasted beans and a gentle swirl of caramel. We barely squeezed into a small table by the window, and as soon as I took a sip of my latte, I felt both my best friends' eyes on me.

"What?" I blinked, lowering my cup, uneasy to take another sip.

Sam smirked. "You can take the girl out of the city, but you cannot take the city out of her coffee order."

Ivy tapped a manicured nail against my cup. "Macadamia milk, a single pump of honey, a sprinkle of cinnamon, and—what was it?—'just a whisper' of hazelnut?"

Sam feigned a gasp. "How very rustic of you, Wren. How positively grounded."

"You two are just jealous your taste buds are uncultured," I sniffed dramatically, taking another sip.

"Uncultured?" Ivy raised an eyebrow. "I drink black coffee, Wren. Sam drinks gasoline."

Sam, unbothered, nodded. "It's true. The stronger, the better. If it doesn't make me see God, what's the point?"

I rolled my eyes, but I couldn't stop smiling. I had missed this— the teasing, the easy banter, the way they saw every part of me, flaws and all, and loved me anyway.

***

I snuck around the corner, my camera steady in my hand. I slowly adjusted the lens, twirling it until my subject was focused. I loved the chase of the perfect moment. It's what made me love my job.

I let my fingers find the shape of the back button to change my f-stop slightly. The dusty antique shop was dark, but it truly made this shot what it was—raw, *in the moment.*

I shot. The light snap made Ivy look up from the book she was reading. I hadn't taken candid photography shots in a few months, but I knew I needed to do more.

This made me happy.

"Wren," Ivy's expression gently welcomed me toward her. She held a worn, leather-bound book, the pages thick and yellowed by time. She hesitated before handing it to me. "I think you should see this."

I shifted, let my camera hang from its lanyard on my side, and reached gently for the book. I flipped the title page, and the words stared at me like a bold twist of fate.

"A Historical Account of the Arslane Bloodline"

Ivy whispered, "It feels historically accurate from what I remember finding before." She exhaled, "It traces Ronan's family after he disappeared. His siblings went on to have many children." She tried to catch my eye, but I was dazed. "I thought...." She shifted, "Maybe it's a peace offering."

I swallowed, a lump caught in my throat. She was confirming that she *believed* me. That she wasn't going to fight me on it.

Instead, she gave me something *real* to give to Ronan.

I closed the book gently, running my fingers over the worn cover like it was a secret that had been kept for too long.

"Thank you. He will find this most interesting."

***

When I stepped back into the house, Ronan's otherworldly presence overwhelmed me with its invisible strength. I felt him from the moment I stepped through the door—his pacing, his waiting. His life paused when I wasn't nearby, but he'd gone *somewhere.*

And I had to wonder—had mine been paused, too?

I poured out the bottle into glasses of wine and handed Sam his with a straw. He leaned back into his chair, his eye narrowing playfully. He was about to ask something absurd.

"So, Wren," He stabbed at his wine with his straw. "Is Ronan your lover, or what?" I choked on the sip of wine I'd just taken, and my eyes met Ivy's briefly.

"What would give you that impression?" I asked, wiping the deep burgundy from my lips.

"So, he's some stranger, tied to your creepy painting... who is ridiculously good-looking, mysteriously well-versed in 16th-century history. And you're *not* fucking?"

Ivy scoffed, "Sam!" She tossed a throw pillow at him but missed completely.

I could see what was coming next.

"What! It had to be said," Sam's smile widened as he doubled down.

"C'mon. He was here at 7 am," Sam's eyes rolled, "Either he's a morning person, and you're pretending to be because you *like* him." He pushed his glasses up, which he did when making a point.

"Or he was a *leftover* from the night before." Sam sipped smugly from his straw, "You act like I don't watch several hours *per day* of murder mysteries. I notice the details."

Ivy and I looked at each other blankly and burst into chaotic laughter.

✳✳✳

It's amazing how much life there was to be lived in a single weekend. Two days with Ivy and Sam felt like years. Sam hugged me at the front door, promising to visit again soon. But Ivy lingered, her stare dead set again on Ronan.

"Take care of her," she said quietly. A command and a prayer.

Ronan nodded knowingly.

I pressed the door shut, letting my hand linger on the seam. I let out a sigh.

"She isn't wrong, Wren." Ronan stepped closer, "Curses don't break without a price." His eyes darkened as they connected with mine. "And would you pay it, Little Bird? For me?"

Would I?

♫ "Time After Time" – Tyler Ward

CHAPTER 14

Time

The living room was bathed in the candles' amber glow. Their flickering gold washed over the room from end to end. I lit them one by one while Ronan eyed me, curious about what mischievous plan I was executing.

The pillars and tall flame sticks made the room feel sacred, like a sanctuary. The tension and color softened, blurring the lines and transforming the room into a holy painting.

I turned the dial on the speaker slowly. The guitar hummed a melody that sent a chill up my spine. It was a beautiful song, with soul in the voice, melodic runs, and breathy vibrato. This was a masterpiece.

I watched Ronan from across the room. His head tilted slightly, and I could see his mind working on the words and feeling the singer's pain. He was trying to catch the meaning hidden in the spaces of music, the meanings modern people have grown numb to.

His expression was new, like someone who had heard silence their whole life, finally experiencing the soft notes of a guitar or the gentle whistle of a flute.

I slowly watched him fall in love with music, the soft, woven sounds of heavenly notes tickling his heart awake. I saw him feel every word of the angelic singer's voice, experiencing the ache and pain of a love song. It was magnificent to witness it all unravel before my eyes. Ronan was becoming something more than a 500-year-old shadow. He was becoming real.

"This," he murmured, "is nothing like the music I remember."

His brow furrowed, trying to understand. "Music was meant for grand halls and performances—rehearsed, perfected." His eyes widened. "This was—raw, intimate in the most tragically imperfect way."

I cross the room and hold out my hand before I can second-guess myself. "Dance with me."

His eyes lift to mine. He takes my hand without a word. His fingers curl, waiting for me to take the lead and show him how to let go. We sway delicately in the center of the room, the melody wrapping us in its gentle embrace, pulling us in to feel the power of each note. His other hand settles comfortably on my waist, and I press closer, closing the space between us entirely.

I knew which words were coming next, and I lightly sang them, harmonizing with the bass of the soulful singer. His fingers tightened, and his breath hitched at his "Little Bird," singing a song for him while we teased the world with our love.

"Time," he whispered. I barely heard it over the music.

"So much of it... lost."

I tilt my head up, meeting his eyes with mine. "Not anymore."

"You're right." I felt him grip me tighter as if he was afraid of letting go, and I sank into that powerful, clinging embrace.

Ronan's fingers trace a slow path up my back. His touch tingles against my skin. I can tell when he's making another memory, pushing Isolde further away from him. He's pushing her out while holding me.

He leans in, his lips brushing just past my ear. I can hear that his breathing is nervous and erratic.

"Do you know how long it's been... since I've *danced?*"

I didn't need him to answer—I knew. It was in the way he held me now and buried himself in this moment. It had been too long. The concept was just a faint outline in a memory filled with horror.

"I'm here," I whispered, a reminder I constantly gave him while he chipped away at the power of Isolde's curse, busy battling the monsters in his heart and fighting for every moment of his earned freedom.

As the song shifted to the final refrain, I lifted my hand to his face and let my fingers trace along the line of his jaw. He leaned into my touch, pleading with me not to stop. His lips parted, and his breath was warm against my fingertips.

I knew that without a doubt, if Ronan Arslane kissed me now, I would be ruined most exquisitely.

"Wren..." his hand slid up, cupping the back of my neck. His eyes dropped from mine to my lips, a hint of yearning evident in his gaze before I braced myself for my undoing.

His lips met mine and deepened without hesitation. My world tilted beneath my feet as his hands tangled further into my hair, disrupting our form and betraying whatever agreement he'd made to maintain his composure.

Ronan unleashed everything he'd held inside and, without words, confessed his love for me in one moment, with one kiss. He silently promised me eternity, as if it were his to give.

♫ "I See Red" – Everybody Loves and Outlaw

CHAPTER 15

Three Months

"Wren, Little Bird. Please!" He was pleading. Ronan Arslane, a darkened phantom, a scary specter, a ravenous revenant. He was the former lover of a wicked femme fatale who consumed children's hearts and entrapped men with her stunning good looks and even worse intentions.

The cursed knight who betrayed such a monster.

He was now *begging*. Pleading. *Me.*

He pleaded with me not to withdraw or pull away. He was asking for my forgiveness and relief from his obligation to be *honest*.

"I should have told you from the very start." His eyes dropped, and his bravado and confidence faded to a pathetic nothing.

"You're a God damn liar." I slammed the bedroom door, causing the house to rattle with my fury.

Ronan appeared in front of me without opening the door. I scoffed at his audacity.

"You never stop breaking the rules," I growled, out of breath with anger.

"You alluded to a cost. You feigned *knowing.*" I snapped. "You knew all along, and you hid it from me." I swung, and he darted.

I would *kill* him.

"I'd never ask this of—" His eyes began to well.

"It's not your decision!" I screamed, my cheeks burning hot. I slammed my fist again, missing his face by mere inches.

"It was *never* your choice! You are not the cursebreaker." I walked away and turned back around immediately.

"I am!" I slammed the door again, standing in the hall, trying to catch my breath while tears streamed down my face. This was the result of frustration, violent fury, or maybe the blood of a broken heart.

He was *inescapable* in this house.

I needed air.

I ran for the door, my legs hammering down the stairs. He stood, blocking the exit, "Please don't leave, I *can't*— "

"You should have thought about that before you *lied.*" My voice was a scathing whisper.

"I didn't lie, Wren. I made a choice."

My eyes glared into his dark, black soul—the one he'd pretended was coming back to life each time we made love, the one he pretended was growing human with every kiss.

"What choice?" I couldn't wait to hear his excuse. What well-formed lie would twirl off his prose-prone tongue? What poetry would he recite in the name of being right?

What... could it be?

"I wish to remain cursed." Ronan's voice was firm. Final.

"You lie!" I swung again, and he caught my arm, tightening his grip. His composure was fading quickly. I saw the human shell cracking, readying to unleash the monster that had once killed me.

"What kind of life is this?" I ripped my arm from his grip.

I threw my hands into the air, gesturing at the prison that was so delicately disguised as our home.

That's what this house was, our prison. He'd gone from the painting and the Badlands to the few rooms of this house, the two no different from one another.

Ronan didn't want this for himself or for me. If he remained cursed, he would recede into the painting, and I would never see him again. He would sulk and torture himself, pretending that I was better off without him here.

"You think, *Ronan Arslane*, that you are so difficult to read?

That you are mysterious?

That you are a wildcard?" I paused, panting, letting my mind catch up with my mouth.

"But, Ronan," my voice dripped with discontent as I spoke his name. So many times, I'd said it in praise while he worshipped my body or pulled me into a realm of absolute pleasure. But this time, I whispered it, grunted it with malice and incredibly ill intent.

"I know you. Your greatest desire is to live the life that was stolen from you." I sneered. "Your entire existence here is so you can be free." I let out a sigh.

"Ronan, you want *children.*" I stared at him, unflinching.

"You wanted a family and a life," I whispered with an angry growl under my breath.

His stare was blank. His only movement was the subtle rise and fall of his chest as he examined how deep my fury quaked.

"Answer this." I crossed my arms.

"Was any of this real?" A tear fell, and I wiped it away quickly. "Or did you manipulate me into loving you?" The question fell hard onto the floor and shattered the room.

Ronan's pulse quickened as I asked it. I felt his mood shift instantly. The monster had arrived.

His body went rigid as he released a voice thick with violence. I was waiting for him to unleash, but he lowered his voice, maintaining its depth.

"Every moment. Every word. Every look. Every touch with every part of my entire body." He stepped closer with each word until his face was only inches from mine.

"It was all real. It still is real, " he snarled back at me.

I scoffed. "And now that you've validated that I am devastatingly in love with you... That I would shatter this world for you. That I would do anything for you..." The tears couldn't be stopped. They flowed freely down my face, covering my swollen cheeks and eyes.

"I have to *forget* you?" I whimpered the question.

"Like I have never knelt and worshipped your body." I let out a deep breath. "Like you've never kissed me with enough fire that we could burn this town to an ashen wasteland." Another tear fell from my cheek.

"Like the gentle moments of basking in the sun weren't the only peace I'd found in *years?*" My voice quaked in sadness.

These were relentless reminders of how incredibly broken my heart now was.

"How?" I asked, my face torn and tattered with fear and hate.

"How could I not?" A breath.

"How could I not set you free when you've given me this love?" I asked, knowing exactly what I was saying and the decision I'd already made.

"Ronan Arslane, I free yo—"

"Not yet," he whispered, kneeling before me as I stood, my heart broken down the middle. "There's still time left," he wrapped his arms around my waist and buried his head into my stomach, feeling his warm tears melt into my body.

"How long?" I whispered, and the question echoed off the walls of the room, enveloping me in uncertainty.

"A year," he replied, "From when you hung the portrait."

I shook my head violently. "Ronan, that's in three months. That—that's not enough time."

I fell to my knees, my eyes met his, and I cupped his face. "But I love you."

I was pleading.

I was bargaining.

I was denying it.

The grief had knocked me down and had taken the air from my chest.

"Do you... Love me?" I asked

"Never more," He whispered back.

"Then, **Get out**."

✶✶✶

Everything was shattered and broken. This house... a wasteland of regret and devastation. Every scene inside was a reminder of what was fading fast. A meteor on a direct trajectory toward us. Our love was a barren world, a dystopian adventure coming to its ultimate end.

I couldn't push him away forever, but I knew I should. I should tell him to go back into his painting, to make himself scarce while I came to terms with the idea that in weeks, which felt like mere hours, I'd forget his entire existence. I should stop loving him so that I could set him free.

The words I reached for beneath it all, under the darkness of my heart, were replaced with something... darker. I felt angry, but... I was hungry. I didn't want distance, no. I wanted his hands on me, his mouth crashing into my body, and I wanted him to extinguish the fire aching in my chest.

He felt it too: a mutual hatred, not for each other but for the circumstances. He was already there before I could pull him toward me. His hands reached their spot on my hips, and he gripped me with a vengeance.

He curled his fingers, and they dug into me with a pain that made me feel alive. His force was demanding, and his roughness was a welcome change from the gentleness that had defined our lives.

There was nothing delicate about his kiss, nothing soft. He embodies heat and hardened anger. His lips taste faintly of everything we lost tonight and everything that was never ours—the sweetness of love with a hint of the salty taste of loss.

He pushed me backward until we hit the hard plaster of the wall. The impact slammed my body into his, a collision that felt as if we would bring this house down. This was the spot. This was the wall he'd slammed me against that first time. This is where he'd killed me.

Perhaps I'd ask him to do it again—anything that would settle the uneasiness, the restless pain that was buried in my chest.

Anything.

Something.

"Wren," his voice a tattered rasp, "I—"

"Don't talk," I demanded, my voice ragged. I weaved my fingers into his hair and pulled him deeper, "Just... don't."

I kissed him harder, biting his bottom lip until he groaned and his fingers tightened around my waist. His teeth grazed my neck, a soft scrape that sent sparks skittering through my body, leaving me dizzy and gasping.

"Wren," he breathes again.

His defiance triggers me, and I thrust my body forward, knocking us violently to the floor. As we landed, I pressed my forearm over his throat, bracing myself as I fell onto him, the impact pushing him deeper—a place I'd never felt him go—and I let out a sharp cry of pleasure. I craved the pain of now, the reminder that there is also hate in love.

"If you whisper my name again, I'll curse you myself." I lifted off of him and then back down, forcing him to press deeply into me.

"Wren," he called my name, ignoring my demand as if he were praying for my safe return. His defiance shifted me, and I used his body as the weapon it was designed to be. The harder I moved against him, the more I sensed him giving in.

Beneath the caring façade lay a defiant demon, crawling and clawing his way out. He wanted it. He wanted to break me open and shatter the nice porcelain doll he'd kept. And he was teetering on the edge. He just needed a little push.

"Tonight, I'm Isolde," I whispered into his ear as I hovered over him. Within seconds, he had me flipped onto my back and pushed himself between my legs, and I felt his hate seethe and him grow. I saw his eyes darken into empty spaces of nothingness. His hands gripped my throat as the shadow in him took over.

The moment I'd been begging for, I couldn't scream. I couldn't yell. I wanted him to take me like I was the witch who'd cursed him.

And he did, controlling my body with reckless desperation, filling me completely. I fought back, pushing against him, but I was no match for the shadow specter, the cursed revenant.

He won every time—and his grin widened after each instance my body revolted against my command to starve him of feeling my body succumb to his efforts.

It was as if he were silently keeping score.

He brought me to my knees, and his thumb brushed over my lips, swollen from the tears and the panicked kisses. He grinned devilishly. He pressed his thumb against my teeth, opening my mouth, and pushed himself down deep. He laced his fingers into my hair, gripping me tightly, and slowly slid me down further. A growing realization dawned when I didn't flinch that I wanted this war. I welcomed it with an open mouth.

He'd have to try harder, if that were even possible.

He filled me as he surged forward, and I needed air, but I grasped him tighter, moving him in deeper—he'd underestimated me. It felt dirty, all of it. But I had wanted *exactly* what he'd give Isolde. I'd asked to be treated like his witch, not his lover. And he was *delivering*.

He released slowly and, without warning, removed his firm grip, allowing me to control myself over him. He delicately tousled and pulled at my hair while gently caressing my face with his fingers.

His hands served as reminders that he still owned this moment. He closed his eyes, slightly parting his lips, and centered his breathing, drawing the moment into himself.

It sounded like panting, like he'd started to lose himself.

My jaw was numb when he withdrew, but I could still feel the vicious smile I flashed at him—a taunt, a beckon, yet a wild affirmation that he wasn't close to breaking me.

He snarled in defeat as he pushed my disgusting smile down onto the floor, and he lifted me to him with ease. He rounded me and slid his fingers over, teasing me. He'd come to know precisely what would be my undoing. But I forced it back and put my climax just out of his reach.

After all, I was *Isolde*. The tricks he'd used on Wren wouldn't work here. As I held it out of his reach, he nudged inside, pushing his strong hands down onto my back, forming a perfectly angled arch over him.

He thrust forward quickly at the same time that he moved the soft pressure of his fingers. I couldn't fight it off on both fronts. I felt it bubbling up from deep in my core.

I couldn't keep it from him.

I was ready, I was waiting—

"Isolde," he whispered in my ear. And it tore me from the moment. The name made me see red. I slammed my body backward onto him, interrupting his pace and momentum. He was already tearing through me, but I anchored my hips back onto him, gripping him between my legs, taking complete control of our pace, and holding onto him deep and heavy.

I gasped for air, panting erratically. I positioned myself at just the right spot when I felt him rise. His groans always began to waver when he was close.

I didn't let up, and at the last moment before he released.

"Wren," his breath shuddered, my name on the tip of his tongue.

Just before he was there.

I stopped.

I fell to the hard floor, rolling away from him. Ronan's confusion scrambled chaotically across his face as he began to watch intently, panting and unable to catch his breath. His eyes lingered on every movement I made over my body.

I called out my own name as I came rushing down from the ultimate release.

Nearly a minute passed, and Ronan stared at the ceiling in complete silence, his chest rising and falling without uttering a single word.

Once I caught my breath, I crawled up to the bed, but not before I looked at Ronan and panted, barely, "I said, *get out.*"

Ronan ignored my malice, welcomed it with a smile, and followed me into the nest of blankets, clinging to my edges like the shadow he was meant to be.

***

"Could it get any worse?" I lay with my head on his chest. He had a heartbeat. He was alive. I rolled through all of the stages of grief at once. I bargained, wondering if I could live a life like this. Ronan and I, trapped in this house, never to *experience* life.

I wondered if I could keep him as a pet, locked away while I lived my life. I couldn't. That would make me like her, and I couldn't return him to the realm that had harmed him. I'd just healed him back with all of my love; I'd just made him whole.

He let my question sit as if he were afraid to answer me. He massaged his fingers deep into my hair.

"Wren..." I felt my name linger in an uncertainty in Ronan's voice.

"There's more that you need to know." He shifted, and the blankets rustled over us. Moonlight from the window cast beams of light onto his face, highlighting only parts of his features.

I sighed.

"I tried to tell you, but you were... *angry.*" His eyebrow arched mischievously. "The only way to break the curse is through your sacrifice. When it's done, your memories of me, and us, will be gone. Not just the big moments, but everything.

My face. My voice. Even how it felt to love me."

"Ronan, you told me this already." He wasn't making any sense...

"Your life will go on as though we never met. You'll be free, and I'll be human again—but there's more."

"What more could there be, Ronan? This is a cruel end already."

"If you ever start to fall in love with me again... if fate pulls us back together. The curse—" He paused, his words nuanced.

"It won't just take *me* back to the Badlands." His gaze met mine. "It will take you, too."

"But—" I hesitated, "How will we—"

"We wouldn't." His eyes lowered, and I saw shame fill the spaces where no moonlight was on his face.

"We can't..." He placed his hand gently on mine.

A tear slid down my cheek. "So, even if I forget... even if you find again, we can never—"

"Never," he says, his voice cracking with the weight of the word. "I can never let you fall in love with me again. No matter how much I want to. No matter how much it tears me apart."

"Will you—" A tear slipped down my cheek, and he brushed it away. "Will you remember me?" I asked.

"Every day." His groaned. He didn't get to live his life blissfully ignorant. No, his punishment was humanity and the gaping hole left by the loss of his soulmate, his Little Bird. His cursebreaker.

"That's why... I'll never be able to be near you again. I know— If I let myself get too close, I'll risk it all. I can't stop it." His eyes were locked with mine now.

"And if I don't break the curse?" My voice is barely a whisper.

He leans closer, his forehead touching mine. "Then I'll stay trapped. But at least I'll know you're safe. Free."

"And we could stay here?" I asked, my eyes hopeful that this could be the compromise.

"For a while, at least—until Isolde found a way to pull me back to..." His words faded off into nothing.

"What do we do?" I whispered faintly, lost.

The silence settled in for minutes that felt like years, accompanied by the soft whistle of the wind blowing through the old windows and the distant song of a nearby bird. His eyes never left my face as he searched for the cracks. I was certain he wondered if I would be the one to double down on his misery or save him from it entirely.

Save his life at the expense of never having known him or our time together. Walk through the rest of my life, free, yet missing a part of my heart forever.

I sweetly hummed the song that had come to mean too much, the one we'd danced to that night, which felt like it was just yesterday. It had been months. We'd been in this space for months, falling deeper and deeper into this curse of a love.

"Time and time again?" he sang back, his voice cracking under the sadness.

I smiled. "Close enough." I sighed deeply, letting the weight fall from me, and nestled into Ronan's arms.

♫ "Heart of Darkness" – Steelfeather

CHAPTER 16

Loopholes

I called Ivy on video chat.

"I can break his curse," I sighed.

"What—How?" Ivy questioned, pushing her glasses up her nose.

"I have to let him go." My lip quivered, and I knew Ivy could see the pain in my expression.

"Let him... go?" She repeated it back, but as a question.

I sniffled, wiping my face. "I won't remember him, and the curse will... push us apart."

"You won't be able to fall in love with him *again* after the curse is broken?" She confirmed what I didn't need to say. Platonic soulmates were so easy. I didn't need to say what she'd already recognized in me.

"Does the curse return if you do?" Ivy was always so brilliant. She knew things before they'd even be revealed.

"Y—Yes." I stuttered on its truth, but what I didn't tell Ivy was that if we found each other, if our love fought back against this punishment...

I, too, would fall victim to it.

And would go into the Badlands.

"We'll find another way, Wren," Ivy reassured me.

"There isn't one. This isn't science. This isn't in one of your books. This isn't a diagnosis. This is magic, Ivy. Magic." I was cynical and hopeless. Everything shattered at once, and I had no control over how the glass landed or the fallout.

Ivy's expression was hard to witness. Pity filled her eyes. She was empathetic, and I knew my pain affected her as well.

"I'm sorry I dragged you into this. I just..." I paused. "I don't have anyone else to talk to."

I'd realized how small my world had become—isolated here with just Ronan. I didn't have the outlets an artist should have.

I didn't have *friends.*

"You've never dragged me into anything. I go with you... *willingly.*" Ivy smiled, "Remember senior year, Mrs. Voss's English class, when you stood up and gave a speech about her inconsistent teaching style and lack of curriculum?"

I cringed. "I did give that woman a hard time."

"You nearly got us both expelled," Ivy laughed.

"We were relentless." I groaned in nostalgic regret.

"We still are, and if there's a chance—any chance—that we can break this curse without you losing him completely, we'll find it."

Ivy always believed in the impossible, and it made her unstoppable. However, I had nothing left to give. My energy was sapped, and it felt paper-thin. I felt like I could tear at any moment and collapse to the ground completely irreparably.

"There's no magic textbook, Ivy. We can't just *Google* it." I kept my voice steady. "I've already looked."

"Then we'll find our answers. Curses always have loopholes. Their creators weren't criminal defense attorneys. They always left open doors, back doors, and ways *out* in case it backfired. Some intentional, some... *not.*"

"How do you even know this?" I rolled my eyes at her.

"My best friend is fucking a *curse*, I couldn't let her go in blind," Ivy cackled. "And, for research purposes," she added, as usual.

"I'm on my way, but while I'm driving... Start with the beginning. Walk me through everything—every rule, every detail. We'll find something in between the lines."

✳✳✳

Ivy entered the room carrying bags filled with papers and books. She opened her iPad and browsed through photos of Isolde's other paintings.

"I found something," Ivy said as she pushed her way into the room, tossing her bags in every direction without looking. Empty gummy bear wrappers and potato chip bags fluttered to the floor like snowflakes.

"These markings... they're not just decorative. They might be a spell or a ward. It might be what *keeps* Ronan in the painting. You see, Isolde Wyld put them on every one of her pieces."

The door swung open, rattling the bookshelves in my editing office. A portrait I had taken a few years ago lurched violently off the wall.

I jumped, and Ivy stared at Ronan unflinchingly. He appeared disheveled, as if he were fraying around the edges.

"Wren Rivers..." he growled.

"Ivy Holloway..." he seethed.

His eyes darted between us like we were in trouble. "We need to talk. Now." His stare was directed solely at me.

I stood. My heart was racing. I'd never seen him like this. "Ronan, we're just—"

"You're playing with something you do not understand." He was sharp, his tongue cutting through the room's tension. He stepped closer to me, unafraid to let Ivy see the phantom in him.

"Do you know what happens to people who try to cheat her? Those who think they can outsmart her magic?"

Ivy stood, her eyes narrowing at the angry specter. "We're trying to help, not *cheat*."

"Help? He barked and rolled it into a bitter, unrelenting laugh.

"There is no help. There are only her rules, the price, and the punishment that follows." He ran his fingers through his dark hair. "There is nothing else," he repeated, staring into Ivy's face, inches from her.

She twisted her neck in a stretch, her lips plumped, and her eyebrow arched high. Ivy Holloway was about the *only* person in this world I'd be scared for Ronan to go toe-to-toe with. My heart raced as I watched my best friend stand facing the curse that haunted me so exquisitely.

"We're being careful," I whispered, reaching out toward him to settle his agitation.

"No." He demanded silence. "His eyes were engulfed in complete darkness, the golden that I'd come to love faded, and I witnessed him change into the creature born of centuries trapped in shadows and relentless torture. His lips curled back, and he bared his teeth, not human teeth but fangs. Sharp, razor-sharp fangs.

"Ronan, what's... happening?" I questioned, breathless.

He stopped, realizing what he'd done. He'd crossed the line, let the monster he was holding back out for just a moment, and we'd both seen it.

Ivy and I were both horrified, but she was less so.

For the first time, I was terrified of Ronan Arslane.

He backed down and pulled himself back toward the door. "The Badlands are closing in, Wren." His eyes softened.

"Time isn't ours. We have weeks. Not years. It's time you came to terms with it." He looked to the floor. "If you step too far, the Badlands will find a way to take you, too."

Ivy's gaze flicked between us, watching him command me.

"Don't make this harder than it already is," Ronan whispered as he left us in the room.

♫ "Gasoline" – Halsey

CHAPTER 17

The Badlands

Warm, golden light flooded the room. The sheer curtains billowed elegantly in the spring breeze, and a faint scent of honey and daisies lingered in the wind's fingertips.

It felt odd. Almost... *too* bright.

A sparkle from my left hand where a large, ferocious diamond sat planted in an ornate golden setting. *When?* I thought to myself. *When did I get married?*

This room felt familiar, but I couldn't remember exactly where I was. The walls were white, and the polished wood floors were perfect—not a single mark upon the surface.

The distant sound of giggles and laughter from the next room interrupted me, halting me in my tracks. Children. I couldn't understand why, but I knew they were mine.

Aly Anders

"Wren?" A deep, grounding voice called out my name, "Wren Ashford, are you awake and hiding?" It was playful and loving. Its sweet tenure fluttered in my ears and warmed me all the way to my heart.

I peeked into the room where the ruckus was coming from, and two beautiful children sat at the breakfast bar. Their plates were filled with pancakes drenched in sticky syrup that was now playfully splattered across the marble countertop.

"There you are, Mommy!" The small boy smiled, his face gooey and happy. We found you! We won!" The little girl with long, dark locks of slightly curled hair and a missing front tooth grinned widely. She opened her arms, and her eyes begged me to embrace her.

Without hesitation, I swooped between her arms, and she held onto my soul with her hands. I felt everything bad melt away, drip off of me in a way that left me unencumbered by a worry that had lived in the darkness of my mind.

"Where's your father?" I asked as I tapped the little boy's syrup-covered nose. "He's looking for you!" he said with a mouth full of soft dough.

"We saved you pancakes!" The little girl slid a plate toward my side of the counter. The perfect stack billowed steam as if it had just come straight off the griddle.

My eyes caught the man leaning on the door frame. It felt familiar. The lean, the eyes, the gaze. He had a mug filled with creamy coffee, and he extended it outward as if to say, "This is yours."

"Oh, and Daddy made you coffee. He said you're *cranky* without coffee!" The little boy smiled at his father, and Mr. Ashford, Theodore Ashford, smiled back at him and swooped up behind him. "Someone's a little tattle tale!" He tickled him near his neck and ears, and the giggle pierced the room, a delight all on its own.

A sound I could listen to all day.

"I *am* cranky without coffee." I smiled and nodded at him as I took a sip. It was the perfect cup of coffee—a perfect blend of sweet and bold with a slight hint of caramel.

I'd died and gone to heaven.

That's what this was because it wasn't my life. I knew it wasn't my life, but everyone around me believed it was.

It was perfect. If there were a heaven, I'd found it.

I'd found it here with Theodore and our children.

Lily and TJ.

I was content in our farmhouse, on acres of land stretching for miles in every direction, in the bold sunlight that warmed my fingers and toes in happiness.

Theo slid behind me, wrapping his arms around my waist and pressing his mouth to my neck near my ear. "We've been waiting for you, Wren."

The way my name slid off his tongue should have been welcoming and felt natural. But it hadn't. It felt like a snake had hissed it. It felt like a monster murmuring my name in the shape of Mr. Ashford.

Before me stood a man whom my mind had deemed perfection. Now, I found myself ensnared in a nightmare of an ideal world with this perfect man, filled with details drawn from the deepest corners of my mind.

But this wasn't mine, and these people weren't mine. Whoever had designed this illusion had forgotten something important: that my perfect was a shadow, a phantom who had fought for a life with me and survived.

Ronan.

Just the thought of him began to crack and tatter the illusion. My reflection appeared in the far mirror—my face and eyes, yet my expression was hollow. I wasn't Wren; I was another version fading into nothing.

"Everything all right, love?" Theodore's voice was smooth and calm.

His eyes filled with black, and his face contorted into the ghastly visage of a monster before disappearing into the air like smoke.

"Is this real?" I asked, my hands bracing against the counter.

The children were gone. The plates of pancakes, too.

The room's golden glow faded into a cool darkness. A chill transformed my breath into smoky tendrils.

Something is wrong.

"This isn't real," I panted, doubling over onto the ground in pain. My heart clenched inside my chest, betraying me.

Breaking.

"Well, Wren Rivers, that depends on your definition of real." A new voice said. It was soft and seductive.

"Isolde," I said, my eyebrow arched. I knew precisely what devil I was dealing with now.

"So kind of you to invite me to your humble hell." I sat at the counter, eyeing the witch with everything I had.

I'd waited a long time to come face to face with her.

I was unimpressed by her witchery. I knew I couldn't be harmed here. I wasn't a resident of the Badlands. I hadn't been cursed. She couldn't hurt me. I was merely a visitor, and a rude one at that.

Isolde's smile widened when I said her name. My, she was *something.*

I could see why she had so many victims. She was alluring, as if she had her own gravitational pull. Her beautiful face was formed from the youth of the lives she collected, a visage composed of the finest features of her victims.

What part of her was Ronan?

I thought about piecing together the parts of her that I knew weren't hers. Beneath it all was an evil witch who appeared on the outside as she truly was on the inside. I knew it.

"You think there's no way out," she whispered, her voice smooth and sensitive. She breathed the words into my ear, tickling the line down my back. "But Wren, Ronan didn't tell you, did he?" Her voice was steady and radiated an attraction you didn't want to give in to.

I swallowed hard.

Damn you, Ronan. Why wouldn't you tell me everything?

"Out with it, Witch." I'd considered being kinder, but I didn't have the patience for pleasantries.

Her smile was cruel in its beauty. "You don't have to forget him. You can keep every memory—every kiss, every gaze, every touch that made your body tremble."

She tilted her head to the side and snapped her tongue. "Ronan is such an accommodating lover, isn't he?"

I lunged toward her, but she moved out of my reach. "Ah, uh, Little Bird, I'd watch yourself in my house." She wagged her finger at me like a child being reprimanded.

"You can keep it all," She finished.

"And?" I asked, "What's the catch?" I scowled at her. "Another curse?"

Isolde leaned in, her breath warm against my ear. "You'll take his place. Stay here. Live this life with your perfect husband and perfect children. No pain, no struggle. You'll be safe, and Ronan will be free."

The room tilted.

I could keep him in my heart, remembering all we'd had, and he'd be free. I'd give him the life he'd always wanted. It was my purpose. I was his cursebreaker.

Many never find it. They walk the Badlands among the madness of their insanity, and emptiness consumes them.

I remembered what he'd said. Five hundred years and he held on and found his...

"Trapped here, forever?" I murmured in question, not for her, but for me. Could I live this life?

"With him?"

The false Mr. Ashford was my idea of the perfect husband. Was he so bad? Would he treat me well? *Maybe.*

Would he make my body quake with pleasure? *Not a chance.*

"Ah, but..." Isolde taunted me, sauntering around me in a circle that was barely wide enough for her, her moves like silk, like a spider wrapping me in a web I might be unable to escape.

"Not *just* with him." She reached out and grazed her fingers across my cheeks. Her touch was warm and inviting.

"With *me.*"

My vision turned a violent red. She was intoxicating me, letting me get high off of her magic. She was seducing me, like all of her other victims, and I so badly wanted to give in to it.

Why did I want this?

I could feel it deep within me. She was tugging at all my tethers, pulling me toward her, and the pleasure I felt was unbelievable.

She was poison, yet I wanted to indulge. I craved the taste on the softness of her lips. I yearned to wrap my arms around her and pull her to me.

"Don't fight it, Wren," she whispered, her mouth nearly touching mine. "I can make your wildest dreams come true," she said, stepping back.

"I could even *be* Ronan." Her face contorted into the shape of him, and I gasped. The sight of his features tore at my heart. She was a near-perfect version, but something subtle in his eyes was missing.

"Wouldn't you like to be my next portrait?" she asked as her face resumed its original, toxically beautiful form. She ran her paint-covered fingers down my body, tapping all the places where Ronan's mouth would visit, leaving smudges of oily black paint behind.

"One more thing, Wren." She whispered, changing her expression to an innocent beauty with pouty lips and big doe eyes. "If Ivy Holloway doesn't stop digging for ways to allude to my curse, I'll find a special place here in the Badlands for her, too." Her face grew darker, more sinister.

"I've always enjoyed expanding my collection of sisters."

"You *will* leave her out of this," I warned, clenching my fists.

"Your time here is over, but please, Wren, make a decision soon," she teased. "I'm sure Ronan is growing weary of having to satiate both of us every night."

✳✳✳

Ronan shook me violently. I could hear the pain in his voice as he called me back from wherever I had gone.

"The Badlands." I whimpered as I slowly came into my reality.

"She took you?" he asked, panting and checking my body for any injuries.

"She did," I replied, reaching for a cup, a glass, something to drink.

My hand reached toward my face, where I felt the heat of the paint echoing on my cheeks.

"You're getting too close. You need to stop looking for another way." Ronan's expression was fierce. He wasn't walking a line with me anymore.

"No—never mind. I—I'm going back." And as he said it, his eyes darted away from mine, the shame in the decision too heavy to share.

"Going back, where?" I paused, anger bubbling up from deep in my chest.

"There?" I questioned.

"Absolutely not, Ronan Arslane. I forbid it."

He glanced up and smiled.

"Little Bird, do you believe for even one moment that you could forbid me to do *anything?*"

"I don't care if it works. I'm forbidding it. Perhaps Isolde isn't the only one who can control you."

"You are *not* a witch, Wren." He smiled and pressed forward, capturing my mouth in a kiss that felt almost like a goodbye.

"You are hope." He whispered.

I pulled back, remembering the last thing Isolde said before returning me.

♫ "Can't Fight" – Lianne La Havas

CHAPTER 18

Fighting

When I opened my eyes, I was on the living room floor, a mug of coffee shattered beside me. I'd passed out again.

It happened more frequently. I'd fade from this world and dream of the next, presumably the Badlands, a place that haunted me even when my eyes were open. I'd awaken, and a warm sting would infiltrate where Isolde had rubbed her thick oil paint on me. She'd left a mark I may never heal from, one that no one could see.

The terrors that haunted me in my dreams were far more fearsome than anything I had ever faced, save for the simple fact that I was running out of time with Ronan. That was what kept me awake at night. That was what I feared. Not some grotesque monster, not a boogeyman in the shadows.

This incessant magic was interfering.

And Isolde.

That bitch.

She'd threatened everything I've ever loved. She embodied everything I wasn't. And Ronan.

I finally recalled the last part of my visit to the Badlands. Ronan was still... I couldn't bring myself to think it, let alone say it.

I vomited.

"Wren?" Ivy's voice cut through the fog. She knelt beside me, her face filled with worry. "You passed out again, and... you're sick."

"I'm fine," I said.

"You don't look fine." Ivy's hand shot out to steady me as I swayed too far the wrong way.

I opened my mouth to finally tell Ivy the truth: that Isolde wanted us. But the words died before I could speak them. I didn't want Ivy to worry, although I could still hear how Isolde said her name, dripping with malice and evil.

"I'll find a special place here in the Badlands for her, too."

I shook it from my head and started pulling myself off the floor, covered in this morning's breakfast and spilled coffee.

"The curse is just calling. It's getting stronger. I'll have to let him go soon." I admitted it. I hadn't wanted to say it, but I did. Ivy didn't look convinced that this was the only problem.

"It's time for a break," she said. We're pushing too hard."

I nodded. It was time to stop—for good.

The way I felt now, sick, frail. *Defeated.* I let the perfect life with Theodore flutter, though, and for a moment, I felt relief.

Maybe I could...

But, Isolde, what would she have me do? Be her little plaything? Torture me while wearing Ronan's face, forcing me to remember him differently. Would I be able to endure a lifetime of whatever horrors she creates?

She was incredibly creative... I knew it was a trap, but I am not sure why I kept considering it. It wasn't viable, as it didn't keep Ronan and me together.

I had to keep reminding myself that it wasn't the answer.

It wasn't a bargain worth entertaining.

"Wren," Ivy said gently, her hand touching my shoulder.

"This comes from a place of love," Ivy sighed.

"But quit fucking around. What aren't you telling me?"

I opened my mouth to answer, but before I could, the door swung open, and Ronan stormed in, his eyes and hair wild as if he had just come from somewhere else.

"I told you to stop," he growled, his voice deep and commanding. His gaze snapped to Ivy, then to me. "What are you two thinking? Have you no idea how close you are to inviting her into this house and letting her..."

He stopped. Maybe he thought he'd say something he'd regret.

But I was interested in the full send.

"I suppose, Ronan," I stood all the way up off the floor, wiping my shirt with the towel Ivy handed me, "Inviting her here would make it easier for you to be with her."

I stood, squaring my shoulders against his.

"You think—" Ronan started, voice low, dangerous. "That I would lay with her?"

"I don't *think*." My lip pulled up to one side in anger.

"I—"

"Thought I wouldn't find out?" I interrupted him.

"It's—"

"Let me guess, *not what I think*?" I scoffed. "It never is. Five hundred years later, men are still the same. Take what you want, then take more."

Ivy's eyes were darting between us, watching this trainwreck of an argument unravel. A little grin of glee as I handed Ronan some of his bullshit back.

"No worries, she made me an offer." I smiled, the fury behind it entirely on display.

"It seems whatever you do to her in the darkness isn't *good* enough," I slammed the insult into his face.

Ivy choked back a laugh.

"She offered me to take your place so I could stay in the Badlands, and in exchange, I would get to remember our great love." I paused. "This *false* love."

"You're not doing that." Ronan's demand sickened me.

"You won't tell me what to do," I snapped.

"Wren, she's been watching you from the start. She knows your heart the way I do because until I am free—until the curse is broken, I am an extension of her." Ronan confessed, "She knows you the way I know you." His eyes dropped. "Every detail."

"*Everything?*" I clenched my jaw in anger. *This bitch.*

I looked at Ivy. "This," I gestured to our research, "It stops now." I sliced through the room with my command.

"She threatened you, too." I sighed.

"If we keep looking for a way out, she said she'll take you too." I confessed, "That's what I was about to tell you before he barged in."

Ivy's eyes widened. "Let her try," she said fiercely. "I'm not afraid of her. I've been doing some research. There have been *enhancements* in witchcraft since her time."

"You should be," Ronan said softly, "The Badlands aren't just shadows and illusions. They take what you love and twist it into torture."

Ronan was afraid. Ivy was *not.*

"Well then, if she's not afraid, then neither am I," I announced, turning my back on Ronan, his anger seething from every part of him.

Ronan shook his head and left the room, although his shadows lingered as if he let them remain, lingering little spies meant to snitch our secrets.

Ivy smiled at me as she returned to her book, confident as ever—unafraid of the monsters that slowly stalked us.

♫ "Golden Hour" – JVKE

CHAPTER 19

Research

Ivy Holloway, present day.

Something was amiss with this entire situation. No one else seemed to think so, but my gut was never wrong—except when I'd eaten dairy, and sometimes then, it lied.

Once, in third grade, I knew Bobby Harrington had taken my pencil sharpener shaped like a cow. I was so convinced that I conducted a thorough investigation, documenting every piece of evidence until I found it hidden in his locker. That was when I realized I'd never let another detail slip past me again. Not ever.

This wasn't elementary school, and the stakes were much higher than dull pencils. I sat on the floor, surrounded by Wren's scattered notes, pages of ancient symbols, and two books that seemed as if they might crumble if I even considered turning another page. I'd made myself at home, and Hurricane Ivy was making landfall.

I chuckled to myself. *God, I'm funny.*

Wren was asleep, and Ronan was likely sulking in an oil-based paint temper tantrum. I was breaking Ronan's scary *rules*, and comedic humor was my way of softening the trouble I was about to get myself into.

My phone buzzed beside me, but I ignored it. I was too focused on the mess in front of me. There was a pattern beneath this chaos—under the symbols, the rubbings, and the high-saturation photographs Wren had taken. A trick. A small door remained ajar, and I would find my way through it.

There was a rhythm to it. It looked like—"A language!" I hummed.

I leaned closer, tracing the lines with my finger. My heart raced. It wasn't just a single symbol but a fragment of something bigger—a spell, maybe, a containment ward. I'd read about those. They're really quite fascinating.

My fingers moved to my phone, scrolling quickly through the photos I'd taken earlier. One in particular caught my eye—a worn engraving on the back of another painting.

"Gotcha," I whispered, enlarging the photo.

"Why would someone like Isolde Wyld," I muttered, flipping through the pages around me, "An ancient, powerful witch who clearly thrives on control..." I tapped my fingers in a repeated rhythm along the edge of my notepad.

"Be so desperate to negotiate with Wren?" I stared at all of the pieces. I saw the familiar edges that looked like they lined up, but some pieces were so misshapen that they didn't belong. How...

"Unless... you're not afraid of *losing* Ronan," I whispered, flipping faster now, searching for anything to corroborate my thoughts. "But you're just afraid of Wren."

I thumbed through pages of library books, borrowed books, and stolen books whose prices I may have disagreed with.

Oh, relax, I'll give them back when I'm done.

I stopped. It was nearly identical to the symbol in Wren's sketchbook.

"No fucking way."

The room seemed to pulse. Then I stopped again.

"Whoa."

It was an illustration—an old portrait of a woman. Dark skin, sharp features, red lips. She looked exactly like me. I stared, my pulse thundering in my ears. Beneath the image, the name "Holloway Coven" gleamed in faded ink.

I blinked.

No. No, no, no, this is a coincidence. Right? Just because this woman had my cheekbones and my mother's eyes didn't mean—

I skimmed the passage below the image, my hands shaking slightly.

The Holloway witches are a lineage of protectors bound to the laws of magic and love. Only a descendant of the Holloway bloodline can bind a rogue witch.

Only a *Holloway* can ensure a curse is truly undone. My throat was dry. I licked my lips, but it didn't help. This wasn't a coincidence. This wasn't a random moment in history, lining up. *I was always supposed to be here.*

A spark raced up my fingers as I traced the page once more, and I nearly dropped the book. The text beneath my hand glowed— just faintly, just for a second—but enough to make me yank my hand back.

I swallowed hard. "Okay. That's... new."

That's an odd allergic reaction to gummy bear overload.

Because that's what it was—something completely normal, not magic at all, explainable.

Yes.

I reached forward once more, gently pressing my fingertips to the page. The glow flickered as if something deep inside the book were alive.

"Oh *God* dammit," I said,

Perhaps I *had* overindulged in energy drinks and gummy bears, which resulted in a sugar high gone wrong. Or...

"This is some Holloway bullshit," I muttered.

The page darkened, shifting under my fingers. Letters rearranged themselves, ink twisting into words that had not existed before.

In canvas, the weaver's fate is bound.
Til the Cursebreaker is found.
A love in truth undoes the stain,
What's freely given breaks the chain.

My breath hitched. It was all right here.

A curse isn't merely a punishment. It's a tether, a chain binding the caster to their magic. If that magic draws its strength from darkness and control, then love becomes its undoing.

Wren and Ronan weren't just breaking a curse.

They were unmaking Isolde.

I flipped through another page, now desperate, my fingers twitching as the text moved again under my hands, responding to me.

A story unfolded. A Cursebreaker. A man trapped in a portrait. A love that grew despite the curse. And when that love became absolute—when the Cursebreaker chose the cursed man...

The witch who cursed him suffered.
The magic that bound them collapsed.
She withered, devoured,
By the very spell she cast.

"Note to self," I breathed, a tightness in my chest, "Witches love obscure poetry." A snicker grounded me in the denseness of the moment. But knowing this had happened before gave me real, tangible proof that Wren needed to break Ronan's curse.

No bargains or loopholes. Those would only make Isolde stronger.

Isolde was afraid, and those little offerings were desperation.

I could smell it on her.

She was worried about Wren choosing Ronan, so she kept him razor thin, siphoning off any extra at any moment. She dragged him back to the Badlands to break his connection to Wren, forcing him to let her strip him of whatever humanity, strength, and will that Wren had helped him heal.

She would undo everything Wren did for Ronan.

But their love... was rebuilding Ronan faster than she could take, and now they were almost stronger than her.

Isolde was already starting to unravel...

I sat back, the breath knocked out of me. My fingers tingled. My mind was racing. I needed to tell Wren. *Now.*

Even if it meant losing Ronan in the process, even if it meant she'd forget—She had to break the curse.

And then I had to make sure Isolde never came back.

Because I now understood what the magic was telling me. I now understood why the Holloway bloodline had led me here. We weren't just witches; we were the ones who had locked creatures like Isolde away before. That meant I could do it again. If I could find her, I could trap Isolde for good once Wren shattered the curse.

♫ "Beautiful Things" – Benson Boone

CHAPTER 20

Goodbye

I sat comfortably, cross-legged on the bed, watching Ronan move through the room. His bare feet, half-buttoned shirt, and slightly messy hair made him appear softer and humbler.

He was fully human in a way I hadn't recognized before.

He caught me staring, my amused gaze lingering on him. A hint of a smirk tugged at the corner of his mouth.

"What?"

I shook my head. "Nothing."

But it wasn't nothing. It was everything.

He felt more like home than this house ever had—more than any house ever had. His smile was a lighthouse when I was lost at sea during a storm. The rhythm of his heartbeat was the measure by which I timed my life.

"Come here," he said softly, holding out his hand.

He spun me around like we were at a grand ball.

"There's no music, Ronan." I rolled my eyes, smiling as I pointed out the obvious.

"We can make our own, then." His mischievous smile curled as we began stepping through the room in a slow dance.

His hand rested gently on my lower back, and our fingers intertwined, tingling where they pressed together.

"Our bodies make magic," he murmured. He was in rare form, a light in his eyes, his face bright with something untouchable. He was on the cusp of freedom—why wouldn't he be thrilled?

My smile wasn't as bright. Dimmed by the knowledge of what tomorrow would bring: a goodbye, a final kiss, and a memory filled with nothing but ghosts.

I didn't know about him, but there was a subtle ticking in my ear when I allowed myself to forget about tomorrow. Like a clock, it reminded me that time was finite. That my love for Ronan would eventually run dry, and I would be left alone again in this world.

"Do you think it will hurt?" I asked quietly as we swayed delicately in front of the fireplace. There was no music to guide us, just the beating of two hearts and the subtle noises of life.

Ronan's fingers traced over mine, the small snaps of electricity confirming his earlier statement. *Magic.*

"No," he reassured me with a smile. But his eyes showed a glint of concern, like he knew better. "You'll forget. It'll be like waking from a dream."

"And you?"

His breath caught. He looked away momentarily toward the fire, the amber flames reflecting in his eyes.

"I'll remember."

My lip quivered at the thought—at the idea that he would get to live his life here, remembering me, us. This.

It almost didn't seem fair. But wasn't that what sacrifice was? Giving something away for someone else. On behalf of them. For them.

I couldn't be mad, but I was jealous. Envious.

I felt him shift our dance, pulling me closer and closing any space between our bodies. He grasped me firmly, lifting me toward him, my legs wrapping around his waist.

His slow steps toward the pile of blankets, the way he nipped at my neck—it unraveled me. I laced my fingers through his hair and pulled his mouth to mine. I kissed him with a promise that I would never love anyone the way I loved him. I kissed him with a plea that, no matter what, he would find me and love me from afar.

I kissed him goodbye, but couldn't say that's what it was.

He tipped us onto the bed, and when we landed, cushioned by cotton and faux furs, he brushed my hair away from my face.

"Wren Rivers," he whispered, "what do you desire?"

I raised my eyebrow and smiled. If this was the moment I had, I would embrace it instead of fearing a moment that hadn't happened yet.

"I want you to read to me," I whispered.

"Oh?" His eyes brightened.

I grabbed a tattered journal from my nightstand and stretched across the bed. Ronan's gaze memorized the contours of my body, his eyes flickering with a hunger I knew too well.

I am certain he had other intentions, but this was my choice.

I handed him an unnamed book. The poems inside were all written by me long ago. They weren't good, but it wasn't about the words; it was about letting Ronan anchor me in this moment.

I wanted to be here.

"Read to me, Ronan Arslane."

***

He recited the words I'd written for hours, pacing himself over each syllable. They were composed long before I knew him and understood what I was searching for. But now, with his voice wrapping around the words, they felt as if they'd always belonged to him.

I watched how his mouth moved and let his voice be the melody that soothed what ailed me. I also noticed how his fingers brushed over the pages and how he held the book like a delicate thing.

I'd told myself we'd go slow. I'd promised that tonight would pass like a dream. I hadn't wanted the chaos we so often thrived in. I tried to deny the madness that cracked open the world when we made love.

But this was our last night together, forever in any existence.

It felt wrong to deprive my body of what it so desperately craved. It wanted one last night. I wanted to be split open and to feel everything. I wanted to remember what I was giving up and to damn God for being so cruel.

I couldn't let this night be a façade. A shield that blurred our truth into a lie. No. It couldn't be that.

I rustled the blankets for the first time in an hour, and he paused his reading. "I thought you'd fallen asleep," he said.

"No, I was just *wandering* and listening to your voice."

"Where did you go, Little Bird?" His voice was tired from reading.

"If this curse..." I started, and his eyes grew darker.

"If the circumstances were different—" I changed my approach.

"Would we be together?" The question was serious, but I could tell Ronan was confused. "What does *being together* mean in this world?" He asked carefully.

"Would we be betrothed?" I asked him. "Would you marry me? In a church, surrounded by our closest friends and family, maybe our goats. Would you take my father's dowry and ravage my body to consummate your vows?"

He smiled.

"What makes you so sure we'd live in my time?"

"I'd fancy the dresses, methinks." I teased.

"Wren Rivers," he crawled over top of me, pressing a kiss to my lips. "You are absurd," he murmured, stealing another. "And I would undoubtedly ravage you on our wedding night."

I smiled, imagining Ronan with a job as my husband—hilariously herding goats and chickens, playing with our children in my time or his. It truly didn't matter.

But his voice suddenly cracked my daydream.

"And, perhaps, I'll ravage you now, methinks," he whispered in that low growl that drove me wild, a tone laced with shadow, as though the phantom within him still lived, the only connection to the Badlands.

His lips grazed my neck, sending my back arching at the mere insinuation of his plans, the fire within me burning and inviting him in to be ignited.

Maybe, if we burned hot enough, a memory of him would sear into my skin, a memory that no curse could take.

✷✷✷

The ashes left in our path resembled a hellscape. Ronan and I had destroyed our room. The fire had jumped and begun to lick the walls with flames. The plaster and ceiling beams became engulfed in a surreal blaze that shattered our world. The smoke wrapped around us like a cloak of darkness, tickling our skin and urging us to unleash.

The painting hung above the mantel, missing its shadow, untouched and protected by the curse. Unburned. Unscathed.

Mocking us.

We crashed into walls, taking bites out of one another, praising the pleasure that culminated just below the surfaces of our skin. He was relentless in his search to sedate me with euphoria, and I... was stubborn. I pushed back. I demanded more. I needed more.

His grip tightened. It should have been too much. It wasn't.

We were beyond the point of pleasure now—we were transforming into something else, something darker that was out of our control.

Ronan pressed himself against me as our room slowly burned to the ground, destroying the house we'd made home. Falling beams shot out hot coals that stung our skin, but we paid them no mind as they landed against us like dying stars.

We didn't care.

We *couldn't* care.

By the time we hit the ground—tangled and shattered—the walls screamed. The flames had already consumed the ceiling and sought anything left to devour, the still-hungry glow sweeping the room with heat.

Sweat poured from our bodies, sizzling as it fell onto the scorched remnants of our bed and room. The destruction we'd caused... proved that our love wasn't just ruin. It was sorcery. The kind that shattered worlds.

The walls' searing screams were dampened by the swirling, suffocating smoke. The room hissed as the flames slowly died, and the floor was devoured like a lit hot coal. Its embers pulsed, waiting, wanting—like they knew we'd do it all again.

The overwhelming smell of charred memories danced between the tendrils of smoke that toiled through the air, in a room now clouded with a familiar darkness.

Ronan Aslane was the devil. I was sure.

But perhaps, so was I.

Looking at this room, I see the damage. The broken parts I will never fix. It had all but burned away, yet I rose unscathed.

I was merely a devil in disguise, and I wondered if I had ever truly been human at all. Not after this. Not after him. No curse could take this from me. Not the fire, not the darkness. Not the way his name felt like power on my tongue. This was mine. And it would linger—smolder—long after Ronan was gone.

♫ "Back From The Fire" – Gold Brother

CHAPTER 21

Sacrifice

The Aftermath

This house feels wrong. Hollow. There is nothing here for me. Not anymore. I started a fire, but I watched it starve of oxygen and die slowly, coming to rest as an amber glow of dark ashes. He's fading too fast for me to hold on. He slips through my fingers when I reach out to catch him.

I'd promised to find him. I said it, those words, I knew I had.

"I will catch—"

I don't want him to go.

He's leaned against the door frame, his shadow whispers, "Little Bird," taunting me with a time when he was mine.

Why did I listen to Ivy? Why did she tell me this would work?

I could feel his kiss, his mouth.

God, I could feel his mouth.

I was his Cursebreaker.

And my burden was the curse of never having loved him. A bitter end, one that I deserved. Living a life of nothingness, wasting away behind the lens of a camera. Fleeing into the night from my problems, a heart barely broken by someone unworthy of my love.

Running from myself.

I closed my eyes, and we were intertwined together, our bodies one.

I blink, and the memory is gone, unreachable.

I closed my eyes as his hands wrapped around my throat, preparing to devour me with his darkness.

I open them, and the pain I shared with him disappears. A hole, a gaping hole where my love once was.

The past drags me under.

Breaking The Curse

The world had already begun shattering around us. We were in reality, yet the Badlands were encroaching. The tendrils of the darkened world snapped chaotically at the edges of Ronan.

They wanted him. The floorboard snapped, sending splinters ricocheting off the walls. The plaster burst under the pressure, caving in around us. There was no time left.

We'd failed to find another way.

"You don't have to do this," Ronan said as he held my hands in his, as if they were fragile. "Wren—please."

Tears streamed down my face, burning and intense. My sadness was the only thing that could provide warmth as the room descended into icy darkness. Our breath billowed from our mouths, laced with delicate frost.

I was already losing him; I felt it. Strand by strand, he was pulling himself from my mind. Not intentionally. *No.* Isolde was taking him back. *Permanently.*

He'd be gone even if I chose not to break this curse. There was no other choice. Isolde had made sure of it. The Badlands were preparing to reclaim him the moment our clock ran out.

It was all too much, too real.

I needed an anchor, a tether. I needed to ground myself in everything holy to break his curse. I searched for a memory, for a tangible moment encased in perfection. And I found him.

That night.

I closed my eyes, and I'm not here anymore.

I heard his words, *"And I'm scared* I won't get to keep you."

His fear was a new human concept he hadn't learned to process. He was still fighting with his humanity, learning how to bend this world to his will.

We're tangled in sheets and shadows, his body pressed to mine.

That night, I could taste the memory on my lips—the sweet tang of his surrender to me and the way he catered to my every desire.

He'd discovered that I was his salvation.

Cursebreaker—he called me. And I saw it in his eyes, the hope. For the first time in his tragic life, he had hope, and it motivated him to worship my being like the church to which he'd sing prayers. He prayed with his mouth, begged with his hands, and laid himself against my softest parts in an all-powerful devotion.

He whispered things too softly for the Badlands to hear. Something Isolde could never take from him.

That night. There was no pain. There was no hurt or ache.

The way his body moved over mine, his hands dragging down my skin, suggested that his form wasn't fully human. He was still a velvet painting that I'd let into me.

I'd let the devil devour me, and I had wanted it.

God, had I.

I needed Ronan just as much as he needed me. I needed to be loved with the feral anger of a cursed knight. I craved the volatile nights of violence and hate. I needed him to push me to feel. Ronan taught me how to live this life: to taste every minute of it, to demand and command what I wanted, and to settle for nothing.

I couldn't do it without these teachings. I would be a husk, an empty little thing. I would be broken.

I opened my eyes at the thought, and he smiled, "I loved that night too, Little Bird."

I looked down at his mouth, our foreheads pressed together while the world tattered and tore around us. The realms blended and ripped into one another. Reality wanted so badly to win, but the engulfing darkness of a realm ready to claim the light was far more powerful.

"There's no other way," I whispered. "You know,"

He shook his head, his jaw clenching under my fingers. "I don't care. I'll stay in the painting for eternity."

"And you will die there." It was harsh. "You'll rot in the darkness, Isolde's little *servant*. She'll chew you up and spit you out. Claim you and ruin you."

He stopped breathing. He knew I was right. I could see it in the subtle grimace on his face. "Then it shall be so, just—don't do this."

"Ronan Arslane," I set up the spell. I knew what to say; Ivy had instructed me down to the perfect cadence.

"No—don't," he gasps, his eyes wide, wild. His fingers dig into my shoulders, his grip almost painful.

"I love you," I whispered. The chaos paused for a moment, a gift bestowed upon us. "Are you sure?" he begged, his eyes welling with tears.

"Never more," I whispered into his ear and kissed him.

It wasn't soft or gentle. It was a kiss full of fire, desperation, and grief. Our unraveling of every moment we'd ever had left us trembling as the roar of the ripping worlds returned. Plaster and dust fell around us as our worlds collided—his with mine.

This curse had waited long enough.

"Ronan Arslane," I say, my voice wavering, but I force it steady.

"I call the curse that binds you by name.
By blood, by shadow, by flame—be broken."

Isolde's haunting voice lingered in the back, a distraction.

Whatever she'd done or said... She was targeting me.

My chest suddenly felt like it had split open, a searing pain so sharp it knocked my next words from me.

"Wren, listen to me. Don't say another word." His voice cracked, *"I'm begging you—please."*

I couldn't let her have him—I had to.

"No—no!" Ronan's scream rips through the room as I push forward, my words rising like a song. His arms tighten around me, forcing my heart back into my chest. Isolde is ripping me apart, slowly tearing me into pieces.

"By the light of the waking world, I sever the chains that bind you. May the Badlands relinquish their hold."

I forced the final words. *The ending.*
Ronan gripped me as if his hands were made of iron. I felt him trying to anchor himself to me. I knew he'd let the magic tear him apart before he would let go.

"Be *free*."

They were barely a whisper. I pushed his hands away from me, breaking his hold and drifting aimlessly into a bright, welcoming light.
A wisp of a violent scream from Isolde rose and then faded.

The chaos paused. One heartbeat. Two.
"I'll be waiting," I whisper softly, the last gift I could give him.

And then he was gone.
The only evidence that anything had happened here was the ringing in my ears and the memory of a scream that had faded away. I'd thought for a moment that the curse had failed because I could still see his shape, his face. His smile.
But the curse hadn't forgotten, and within minutes, it began to take everything away from me.

♫ "Lost Without You" – Freya Ridings

CHAPTER 22

Hollow

"Earth to Wren—" Sam waved his hands in front of my face, snapping his fingers for effect.

"Sam," I shot him a glare, "Good morning, *Missile Control.*"

The day was already moving at full speed, and I wasn't even in orbit yet. I felt rushed, as if I were late for something that didn't exist. I had walked here, but I couldn't remember the walk itself—only flashes of light, the cold bite of morning air, and now, somehow, Sam's kitchen.

"I haven't had enough coffee." I rolled my eyes, trying to pull myself back into reality.

Without missing a beat, Sam slid a paper cup over from across the counter and kicked out a smirk and a dramatic faux hair flip.

"Ma—"

"Macadamia milk latte," he mimicked my voice perfectly. "A shot of hazelnut, one pump of honey, a sprinkle of cinnamon..." He paused, his eyes sparkling with mischief. "And a splash of existential dread."

"*Houston*, you're the problem," I whispered as I sipped the perfect coffee.

"Ok, Space Cadet," he leaned casually against the counter. "I hear Mars is fresh out of two-bedroom, one-bath condos," he snarked. "But I have a reliable lead on a downtown loft with 'high-powered photographer' written all over it."

"For your *other* photographer friend?" I raised an eyebrow.

"Wren, please." He wiped up a splatter on the counter that wasn't there. "We both know you and V are my *only* friends."

Sam gave me an exaggerated pout before glancing down at his phone.

"Is Ivy coming?" I asked, swirling the cup while my eyes caught the distant flutter of shadows in Sam's kitchen.

"That witch—with a capital 'W'—" Sam pushed his glasses up the bridge of his nose, "already flew back to Japan. Can you believe her?" His eyebrows shot up in exaggerated shock.

"Wait—she didn't say goodbye?" I questioned.

"Right?" Sam spun around dramatically, throwing his hands up. "No goodbye. No emotional send-off. She ghosted us, Wren. *Rude.*" He smirked.

I tried to laugh, but it didn't come naturally. I couldn't help but feel a little unsettled that she would leave so abruptly. I didn't even know she was considering going back to Japan.

"Do you think she's mad at me for something?" I blurted it out. Best friends didn't need goodbyes, but something in me felt like this was a maneuver. She was telling me something.

"Uh, no, it's just Ivy being... Ivy," Sam brushed off the concern.

"Good for her," I said, feigning support. "She deserves a little adventure."

"That girl lives a full-blown manga romance, Wren. Her life is the adventure." Sam continued doom-scrolling across multiple platforms.

A silence split the conversation.

"You're extra needy today?" Sam looked down the bridge of his nose, his eyebrow arched in humor, questioning me.

"Can I bring him?" His eyes filled with uncontainable excitement.

"Oh god, **no**." I shook my head rapidly.

"Oh, c'mon, *he should come*," Sam's grin spread wider.

"No, absolutely not," I repeated.

"Too late—I decided, and Ivy gave me her vote by proxy, so you're overruled, and I say, *he's coming.*"

His voice faded as he strolled into the darkness of a faraway room, and then he returned to the room with the giant stuffed hippo.

Mark.

We meet again.

We'd won him on our *only* date back in the early 2000s.

"Mark is ready to snoop in people's closets!"

This man had *issues.*

✷✷✷

We walked down the city streets together, carrying a three-foot-tall stuffed hippo. I dodged the odd looks and stares while Sam soaked it all in. Despite the humiliating scene, I hadn't laughed that hard in weeks, maybe even months.

Mark had a way of doing that.

***

It had been two months since I sold the house—the house that had been everything and then nothing in the blink of an eye. One morning, I woke up, and the halls felt empty. The walls weren't mine, and the rooms felt as if they belonged to someone else.

The rooms that I once knew felt like home had turned hollow. A different version of me had decorated them. I didn't live in that house anymore. I painted over all the vibrant colors, washed away any trace of my presence, and sold it to a cute couple expecting their first child.

Maybe they'd call it a home after a while.

I stood dead center in another seemingly perfect loft. The windows allowed just the right amount of light to enter, and the sun's beams darted around, bouncing off each wall and reflecting toward another. It was as if I were in the center of the universe.

I stood in the center of the room, the point where all beams connected, and I absorbed the heat, the warmth. It embraced me in a way that made me feel a little less empty.

A little less lost.

After the house was sold, I returned to the city and stayed with my parents for a while, but Sam pulled me out of the catastrophe that was my life.

You know, I'm thirty and living at home with my parents. I have a struggling photography career and virtually no dating prospects. I lead an empty life, similar to this vacant loft, where the echoes of our footsteps reflect the echoes of my failures and shortcomings.

Tap. Tap. Tap.

It taps away at my mind like a reminder I don't need.

But I had to push through the emptiness, knowing it would only be temporary until it was filled with parts and pieces of my next chapter.

I'll fill it with:

my furniture and hopes.

My art and dreams.

My friends and laughter.

Yes—absolutely—this loft was another fresh start. It was another second chance. But it felt scary, like hope after having been broken too many times before. I ran my fingers over the surface of the wide counter in the kitchen. The marble was flawless. This was an entertainer's loft.

I could see the parties, trays of appetizers, and dainty little cocktails floating around on trays. I saw Sam singing karaoke in the living room, taking advantage of the incredible acoustics.

Much like he was *currently.*

I stared a hole through Sam's chest, and just before he tried to hit a high note that his vocal cords weren't meant for, he stopped.

"What? Bitch, act like you're not going to sing here." His face grimaced at my judgment as he wandered off to snoop through the closets.

Is this where I wanted to start living again? Is this where I intended to claw my way out of the darkness that had shadowed me for weeks? I hadn't told anyone, but it felt as if I had just awakened one morning, and my heart was broken for no explainable reason. I was simply shattered.

Not—*they're* out of macadamia nut milk, but have oat milk *broken*, but truly shattered. As if the world had betrayed me in my sleep, breaking my heart into a million pieces but forgetting to tell me that it had.

Imagine waking up and not knowing *how.*

Or Why?

But there was something, and there was no logic, no information, no fact to explain it. I kept searching—inside every loft, every morning coffee, every familiar face—for something I couldn't name.

"You okay?" Sam asked, his eyes narrowing as he stepped into my view. He suddenly broke the trance I'd thought I was in.

I was crying. I hadn't realized it, but I wiped my face with my sleeve to conceal the evidence.

He reached out and clicked his mouth, "Oh honey-baby, it's not that nice." He joked, but his embrace said the words he didn't need to say.

"I'll take it," I said, surprising myself, but I didn't want to walk into any more soulless lofts and apartments, trying to find what was missing. It was pretty clear after the tenth version that I was looking for a *phantom.* I just wanted this part to be over to start moving forward. I was tired of standing still.

"Are you sure?" he asked, slurping from the iced coffee that was nothing more than ice now. "We can keep looking. I don't want you to settle." He shook the cup, and the rattle of ice echoed throughout the quiet room.

"This is the one, Sam," I smiled softly. I knew he'd look at a thousand lofts until I found the perfect one.

"It's the best one we've seen. It doesn't smell like a dead animal, and the light is magnificent." I paused, looking around again. "I can see... I can see myself happy here, I think."

"Girl, for what they're asking, this place better tuck you in and read bedtime stories." He mumbled it as he wandered to the far window, hands on his hips, looking out at the skyline.

"Well, it is a vibe," he said, his voice booming in the emptiness. "Could use a little personality, though. Maybe some plants. Or, you know, a soul." He snickered, delighting in his own humor.

"Plants," I agreed, wiping my face again and sniffing away the last of the unexpected tears. "Definitely, plants."

"Ok, it's growing on me. I like it too." he confessed, a sparkle in his eye when he saw the smile on my face.

♪ "Beyond" – Leon Bridges

CHAPTER 23

A Second Curse

Ronan Arslane, present day.

I started walking in the evenings a few months ago. Something about the buzz of a city alive in the darkness excited me. There weren't cities like this when I was human, having a life that spanned so many years; however, being indefinitely void of the knowledge that came with the current-day calamity was chaotic.

These walks quieted that maddening clatter. The people-watching, the cool night breeze, and the way the sky remained in a twilight hue from the bright reds and oranges that blended together.

I walked by the glow of another nondescript building, but something compelled me to pause.

Stop.

Frozen in my path, unable to lift my foot.

Accented by the soft, ambient amber glow of candlelight, that was her.

Wren Rivers.

This wasn't the first time I'd seen her. I often tried to visit from afar, but this is the first time I've seen her unexpectedly. She looked like a dream or a painting. Her edges were smooth, and her light burst from the darkness of the background. She was always the focal point. I always lost myself in the few fleeting moments when I could stop long enough to let my eyes linger.

I registered her expressions and cataloged her smiles. I judged whether she was happy, despite her lack of memories of what we had endured together.

Tonight, she was. It was in the slight crinkles of her eyes when she laughed, the ease of her smile, and the fact that the dress she wore clung perfectly to her every curve, as if it were curated for this moment—like she intended to be unwrapped, like a gift.

And it ripped through me, my heart, cleft in twain.

She tilted her head, her smile magnetic as she intently absorbed whatever story the man across from her was telling. That same man leaned in closer, his hand resting casually on the table between them—an offering.

I recognized him immediately. With his slicked-back sandy hair, ice-blue eyes, and squared jaw, he resembled a modern-day prince.

Ashford.

My jaw tightened as I stepped further into the shelter of the street lamp.

I knew this story. It had been written for her long before she brought me into her house and placed me above that mantle. This was the life the Badlands had promised her—a world without darkness, without curses, without me.

Wren had told me about the twisted illusion Isolde crafted for her, using parts and pieces of her own mind—her deep desires.

A house, a family, a picture-perfect husband who erased me from her mind and heart. Wren had told me it wasn't real; that the life the Badlands had shown her wasn't what she'd wanted.

I believed her.

But, *maybe*. She did not want to break my heart.

Theodore smiled and leaned closer again, causing my breath to hitch and my heart to pound. It was killing me.

Wren laughed softly, her shoulders relaxed and her lips parting in the familiar way that drove me wild. The way they did when she considered how she would devour you later.

I stood outside, enveloped in the rush of the city, yet that laugh echoed in the walls of my memories. It used to be mine.

I sighed, taking a moment of silence and calm for the love I'd lost and the life she'd found, for the happiness that filled the void left when our lives were ripped apart.

She'd found someone else. Someone new.

I stepped out of the shadows, relinquishing her, setting her free, but condemning myself.

I closed my eyes. I wanted to stay by her side and watch her happiness unravel. I wanted to watch her live her life, but this pain... I couldn't. I turned to go, but not fast enough to miss how her fingers brushed across her wine glass. Her eyes flickered toward the window as if she'd seen me there. Her gaze met mine, allowing our eyes to connect in a momentary acknowledgment.

The subtle insinuation in her lips looks like the start of a smile.

Or perhaps I was seeing something that wasn't there. To her, I must have been just a shadow that caught her eye and nothing more, for she looked back toward him—toward her future.

♫ "Electric" – Alina Baraz, Khalid

CHAPTER 24

Lost

"I've been back for three years," I smiled, swiping across the glossy screen of my phone, "and I have never seen this part of the city." I looked up at the buildings and skyscrapers that floated into the clouds. I was in awe.

Old Wren, who flew to a sleepy town to escape her deadly, violent ex-lover, would *indeed* be panicked.

I'd crossed over three streets and turned left twice.

I stood once more on a street I was certain I had visited before, but now, less worried about being late and more focused on the intricate details of the sky and buildings, I grabbed my camera and, with one hand, snapped a few shots that captivated me.

I looked around one corner and then up at a glaring street sign.

"Vernon!" I laughed, "I'm supposed to be at *'Arnold.'*"

I grabbed my phone and left a message for my client: "Hey, going to be a little late. I'm unsure who named all these streets after old men, but I got turned around. I'll be there soon." I hung up.

I'd just bought myself a few minutes to *explore*.

I strolled down an empty side street, unafraid of anything that might lurk in the shadows.

"You look lost," a deep voice says from beside me. "And pretending not to be."

I glance up, ready with a snarky retort. People in the city never minded their own business; it was part of what I loved about it. The words caught in my throat, and I let out a cough. I quickly sipped my coffee to buy myself a moment, but it was empty. How tragic.

He stands there—dark eyes, tall, broad shoulders that look like they once carried the weight of the world on them. There is something almost familiar about him, as if I'd seen him before in a dream or a movie.

"Depends," I say, recovering from my awe-struck daydream. "Are you offering directions or judgment?" I smiled and looked up at the street sign above his head. He casually leaned against the brick building.

His lips curve into a slow smile that feels like it belongs to... *me*.

"A little of both."

"Fair." I tilt my head, wishing it weren't rude to grab my camera and snap a thousand photos of his perfect jaw and infinite eyes. I am not often enthralled by a perfect stranger, but something is haunting about him.

"I'm—I'm looking for *Arnold—Street*." I pause and look down at my phone again. "No—*Boulevard*."

"Are you sure?"

"I've never been more sure." I clumsily juggled my phone and an empty coffee cup.

"Someone must be playing a trick on you," he replied, chuckling, "There's no Arnold Boulevard, not in this city."

"There isn't?" I raised an eyebrow, "Well, shit." I laughed.

I've had clients back out for every reason, but providing me with a fake address was a first.

"Then it seems I've been stood up." I spun, looking in every direction. "What are the chances you know of a place to get a good cup of coffee?" I shook my empty paper cup and waited while he slowly considered my question. I tilted my stance in amusement; never had anyone thought so hard about coffee.

"I do," he says, crossing his arms casually. "But it's not on any map."

I scoffed. "What is it, a *magic* coffee shop?" I realized my question felt flirtatious without even trying. *What was I even saying?*

"It's not far from here."

I shot him a skeptical glance. "How convenient."

"It is." His eyes squint slightly as he extends his hand. "Ronan."

The moment our fingers touched, static snapped, and for a split second, it looked like an arch of magic between our hands. His fingers lingered as if reacquainting with an old friend, and I pulled back quickly.

I shook it off, static. *It was static.*

There was definitely something off about today. The mix-up with the client address and getting lost. This ominous stranger had me cornered in a desolate alley. I smirked at the dark thought that flitted across my mind.

"Wren," I say, my voice softer now, humbled by the day's oddities.

"Wren," he repeats, and the way it sounds coming off his lips brushes against my neck and sends shivers down my spine.

"Can I call you *Little Bird?*"

"Little Bird, huh?" I smiled. "You'll have to earn that nickname."

"Oh, I intend to."

✳✳✳

As soon as the door cracked, a waft of freshly ground coffee and cinnamon hit my nose. I loved this smell. This place is cozy—warm and comfortable. The afternoon sun filtered through the stained glass sun catchers, casting colorful patterns onto the tables like a kaleidoscope.

"Nice spot," I say, looking around. "Let me guess—you're here all the time."

"I'm a regular." His smile was small as he nodded. He gestured to a table by the window. "This one's ours."

The barista pulls two shots of espresso before I even glance at the menu. The name at the top of the paper card is 'Little Bird Coffee Co.'

"Is that why you called me Little Bird?" I asked, pointing to the menu.

"Ah, yeah, a marketing tactic." He shifted in his seat, getting comfortable just as a barista swooped by like a hawk and landed two perfectly shaped pastries on our table.

"You'll have to trust me," Ronan says, catching my questioning glance.

I raise an eyebrow. "I love your confidence." I set the menu to the side. "It's refreshing," I added.

He leaned back in his chair and pulled his arms behind his head. "I have a super power, Little Bird," he smirked. "I can guess anyone's coffee order."

He captivated me. I was enthralled. I was along for whatever ride Ronan, the stranger from the alley, was taking me on. A day that started with failure had turned into something I hadn't expected.

Those were the best days—days that didn't ache and didn't feel like a piece of you was missing, as if you were just aimlessly wandering, trying to find where you left it.

No, today felt like an adventure, intentional. And it was just the adventure I needed.

The barista set the paper cup in front of me. "Here you go, *Boss.*"

I instantly grinned. "Boss?"

"Ah, yeah, by *regular*, I meant I own it." He smiled softly.

I looked at the cup before me, and my grin transformed into a broad smile. He claimed he'd guessed my coffee order, but without even tasting it, I knew he was mistaken.

"What?" His eyes darted from mine to the cup I delicately thumbed over with my fingers.

"It's smaller than I expected," I said, winking.

He coughed, bringing a napkin to his mouth. His cheeks blushed, and he looked around the cafe chaotically.

I'd cracked the poised stranger who had an answer for everything.

"Size," he whispered, pulling himself over the table and closer toward me, so close that I could feel the heat of his words as they left his mouth. "Doesn't much matter when you're just tasting it." His grin was returned to me, devilish.

And suddenly, I had become a victim of my wit. Ronan was sharp. I was falling behind. I squirmed in my seat, nearly losing my breath.

I held the cup to my nose and gently smelled—nutty, milky, with a hint of cinnamon. *It couldn't be.*

I brought the warm paper to my lips and took a small sip. Ronan watched from across the table. There was patience in his eyes, as if he were waiting for me to enjoy it.

It was warm and creamy. The macadamia blended perfectly with the honey, the cinnamon lingering on my tongue long enough to make me want another sip.

I know this drink.

"Ronan," I brushed my tongue over my teeth, "This... is... disgusting." A smile crossed my face.

"You are a terrible liar." His smile, if it was even possible, spread wider.

"How did you know?" I asked, taking another sip of the perfect cup of coffee, perfected to exactly my liking.

"It's magic, Wren." He said it like he'd known me for years. Like we were old friends having a chat over coffee. Like we were lovers who had spent the night tangled around one another.

"And now I wonder what other tricks you've got?"

"Hmm, well... I dance." He replied. "Occasionally," he added.

"Oh?" I blinked, not what I was expecting.

"Not in front of strangers, of course. But for the right person? Absolutely."

"What kind of dancing? I sipped my coffee again.

"Depends on the night," he says, a slow smile curving his lips.

"Sometimes, I'll even dance with beautiful women I meet in the alley."

My chest tightened. Something in the way he spoke to me was achingly familiar. The way he looked at me, his eyes dropping to my lips as if he'd kissed me a thousand times in another life.

"Sounds dangerous," I say, lowering my voice.

"It can be." His eyes were lingering on mine, that flicker of familiarity drawing me in.

♫ "Vigilante Shit" – Taylor Swift

CHAPTER 25

Hair

Ivy Holloway, after the sacrifice.

I whispered an incantation under my breath, Holloway power coursing through my veins. A small bauble of light flickered at my fingertips. There was a scarcity of that here.

The Badlands welcomed a witch without ties, like I was a prize they could win should I feel betrayed. I took a deep breath. The faint tang of ash and old magic lingered in the stagnant air.

I'd been hunting for years. Three, to be exact. I'd finally caught up to the prey I'd been tracking. The end was near.

For her, not me. For me, this was just the start.

"Come out, Isolde," I called, my voice steady and echoing wildly across the damp, crumbling landscape.

A gust of wind blew back in response, carrying a chorus of screams—tortured souls, many of whom Isolde had likely collected herself.

I felt the eyes on me. The stares and gazes of beings too afraid to reveal themselves sneaked from the shadows under the concealment of darkness. I'd allow it. They'd endured centuries of her torture, of her relentless rule.

They could watch.

Isolde was *lame*. She was slightly shattered. Wren's sacrifice was a critical blow to her power, and she was hemorrhaging it. That's how I'd tracked her. She couldn't stop her magic from leaking out of her body, but I knew she was a snake with many heads. I knew her to have regenerated from the edge of death.

I had hunted Isolde Wyld every single day for three years, and in the Badlands, three years felt like an eternity. I had become familiar with this land and how it had been shaped. I never slept; I barely rested.

We had faced off in the shadows numerous times. We had danced in the night with my blade against her neck, and each encounter taught me a new lesson. Each time, I refined my plan.

A flicker of movement that reflected my light.

"Isolde, is that you?" I chattered her name off my lips.

"Little witch," she hissed, her voice slicing through the silence like a knife. "Come to beg for mercy?" She panted, out of breath.

"Forgiveness?" She added.

I'd found her, cowering in a corner, her back against the wall.

She had grown ugly. Lacking her full strength to alter her appearance, she was now what nightmares were truly made of.

"Oh, that's horrible," I waved my hand in front of my face, "Isolde," I wretched. "Have you stopped washing?"

I stepped back, distancing myself from the grotesque smell.

"If I were to beg for anything, it would be for you to use soap," my face cinched with disgust.

"You've really let yourself go."

Isolde, the old Isolde, was vain. Her youth and appearance were her most prized possessions. They were her only possessions, for her heart was so black and her mind so horrid. She was nothing but a beautiful exterior and a decaying, rotting corpse on the inside.

Her eyes darkened as she shot at me with force.

"Use your *words*, Isolde." I giggled, dodging her advance, my cloak swirling around me.

She laughed, a bitter, cracked sound—something that had died too long ago for anyone to remember.

"You aren't enough, Holloway," she screeched, her voice sounding ancient and broken.

"We'll see." I thrummed as I positioned myself.

She raised her hand, dark energy starting to snap and crackle at her fingertips—but I was faster.

My magic surged, ancient and unstoppable. It sizzled through the air with a golden glow that pierced her shadows.

Isolde stumbled, her eyes wide with disbelief, as I wrapped around her, my chains of binding light contrasting against her fading darkness.

"This isn't your world anymore," I whispered as I stepped closer. "The Holloway Coven sends its regards." I finalized my threat.

My ancestors were the last defense between darkness and the world. Now, after centuries of silence, the Holloway name speaks once more—through me.

With a flick of my wrist, I grabbed Isolde by her hair.

A witch's hair was her pride and joy.

You *didn't* touch a witch's hair.

I grasped her stringy gray locks into a tight fist. I kicked her backward and began to drag her back across the treacherous landscape of the Badlands.

She had spent centuries weaving nightmares, and now the Holloways had come to collect. The entire realm chattered and cheered as Isolde made her last ride.

Isolde's screams replaced the yells of the thousands of tortured souls she'd mercilessly trapped here. I heaved her limp, powerless body toward the rift I'd created to get here.

A portal spell that my grandmother had left me in her notes.

She thrashed violently as we approached the vast crack where light fought the shadows. A familiar gold frame, ornately embellished, awaited, like a gate we must pass through to leave this place behind.

I felt her voice crack under something familiar—fear.

"No—no!" She squirmed, trying to crawl away from me, the dust from the ashen ground covering her body in dark charcoal.

"How fitting," I thought as I watched her paint wrinkled skin with the remnants of her tortured souls, her cursed mementos she'd kept for so long.

"Wait!" Her lips trembled. "Please," she whispered, eyes locked onto the floating frame. "We can start over. I can change."

I knelt beside her, my hand still gripping her hair. I leaned in close, my voice steady. "You're right. You will change—into art."

Her scream tore through the air as I drew the painting closer. The rigid frame, glowing with a hungry light, anticipated her arrival.

"Isolde, I think you will enjoy your new accommodations," I smirked. "It's a prison of your own design."

I hurled her into the painting with a final burst of power. Her body twisted midair, her arm flailing and grasping at nothing that dared to catch her.

Isolde was now a perfect painting, pressed flatly on a cursed canvas.

♫ "Rise Up" – Andra Day

CHAPTER 26

Pancakes

Ivy Holloway, present day.

The poetry section was quiet, nestled in the smallest corner of the bookstore, away from the steady hum of customers near the front. Perhaps this is why he liked it, reading poetry.

It was certainly a sight.

This store smelled like my dreams: old paper, history, coffee, and ink—tantalizing scents that made me long for a part of my old life.

Before the Badlands.

He stood with his back to me, one hand loosely holding a slender volume of poetry, his head bowed in deep concentration.

His fingers traced the words. A human who hadn't been human for so many years had many classics to catch up on. The sun illuminated his face, and I thought I saw his lips subtly reciting the poems under his breath.

For a few minutes, I didn't say anything. I just stood there, watching him. It had taken me three years to get here, and now that I was...

What was I supposed to say?

He looked... different. Entirely human. But Ronan was still there, just deeper under the surface. It was in his shoulders, how he seemed to be hearing some words for the first time, and in a way, it almost felt like the words were asking him permission to exist in such an order.

He turned the page slowly, his eyes flicking across the verses with practiced ease, unaware that I was standing directly before him.

Or maybe not. Ronan Arslane had never been one to miss much.

When he finally glanced up, his gaze fell directly on me.

I didn't move.

For a long moment, neither did he.

We stared at each other—I could see his mind working, the careful mask he had learned to wear slipping for a moment as he searched my face for anything. He was waiting to see if I knew him.

He didn't know.

"Ronan Arslane." I smiled, nodding in acknowledgment.

His posture changed immediately; the tension in his shoulders slid away, and his fingers released the book he had held. His lips parted in a breath of disbelief.

He let out a laugh, quiet and short. "You—You remember?"

I nodded, a small smile curving at the edges of my mouth.

"Every second."

His eyes closed, and when they reopened, they were filled with something I hadn't expected—relief. Not the kind you feel when you've avoided danger, but the profound kind that washes over you when you realize you are not alone.

"Ivy Holloway," he said, testing the sound of it. "It's certainly been a while."

I crossed my arms and tilted my head. "Approximately three years."

He smiled and ran his hand through his hair. "Has it been that long?"

I nodded again and glanced around to see if anyone was listening.

"How—Where have you been?" he asked, setting the book on the shelf and turning back toward me.

"Working. Overseas." I was trying to convey something without fully expressing it.

"Overseas? Really? Anywhere nice?" he questioned sincerely.

I chuckled, "You wouldn't care for it—it was rather... bad." I grinned, and I'm sure he caught the glint of mischief in my eye.

His eyes widened as he grabbed my arm and pulled me to the side, where no one could see us.

"You went there? Ivy, are you mad?"

"It really depends on who you ask," I smiled. "Let's find somewhere private. I have something to show you."

I was giddy and eager, and I wondered if he could feel it, too.

✳✳✳

The café was bustling. There was enough noise for Ronan and me to speak freely. I set the painting on the table between us, still wrapped in a dusky velvet cloth. I had carried it so far that I had forgotten how large it was. When I realized it took up the entire space, I slid it off the table and leaned it against my seat.

Ronan eyed me, and then it cautiously. His fingers tapped against the table once, twice—his only tell.

Controlled and curious, I thought to myself.

I leaned back, arms crossed, trying to stifle the giddy grin that threatened to escape during my big reveal.

"Oh, relax. It's not for you." I teased as I began to pull my cloak off my shoulders. It was warm in here.

"What's good?" I flipped open the menu, examining the long list of too many choices.

"The first sign of probably bad food is a big menu." I ignored Ronan's blank stare, which demanded an explanation from me.

His eyes narrowed. "You can't just bring a painting wrapped in fabric and expect me not to be concerned, Ivy."

"Oh, well, when you say it like that, Geesh," I widened my eyes in frustration.

"I like the pancakes." He raised his brows.

"I did *not* take you for the flapjack type." I chuckled.

The waitress came over to take our order. "You two lovebirds ready to order?" She snapped her gum immediately afterward.

"He's my brother, and we'll take pancakes. Two stacks." I winked at her and sent her on her way.

"Ivy—" Ronan's voice, pleading for me to pull it all together.

I stood and pulled back the painting, lifting the velvet off the painted image.

He instantly recognized the same golden frame. But his eyes fixated on the portrait. I let a goofy smile stretch across my face, knowing I looked like an idiot. But he wasn't looking at me. No, he was staring deep into the eyes of the one who'd scorned him. He was seeing her in her true form, her mangled, hideous exterior.

Isolde's face, frozen and wide-eyed, mouth agape in mid-scream. Her hands pressed against the canvas, crooked and deformed like the claws of a monster.

She was a grotesque little thing.

"I wouldn't know where you'd hang it? A haunted house?" I paused. "She should probably stay at least 100 yards away from children. I don't know all the witch bylaws," I rambled on, but Ronan wasn't listening.

I looked at her, then at him, then back at her, and again at him. I gazed at her and blew her a little kiss.

"Is that...?"

I nodded. "Isolde Wyld. Cursed to canvas. Permanently."

His lip twitched, "Ivy..."

I covered her back up and whispered her a soft, "Nighty-night."

"You—you went to the Badlands... for this? Her?"

"Of course I did." I leaned forward, my voice lowering. "No one messes with my friends and gets away with it." I stabbed my pointer finger down onto the table. Within seconds, two plates of pancakes slid between us. I smiled at the kind woman who even thought to bring me extra syrup.

"She can't hurt anyone anymore?"

"Not a chance. Her power is inert. The curse is gone. You and Wren... you're free."

He let out a breath, and his shoulders relaxed.

He didn't speak, but I was *starved.*

Three years in the Badlands made you long for the fluffy dough of pancakes soaked and drenched in sticky maple syrup. I tore into my stack, unbothered, perhaps even slightly unhinged.

"I'm sorry," I let it fly, the apology I'd wanted to let out since the bookstore. If I said it while my mouth was full of pancakes, did it distract Ronan from how awful a friend I was?

"I should have done it sooner. I thought there was more time to find another way. I failed her, Ronan. I could have saved her memories—"

His hand stretched across the table, enveloping mine. He felt warm, grounding, and steadier than I had imagined.

"You didn't fail, Ivy, *God,* you *are* mad.*" He laughed.

"You gave her a life, a chance to be whole. She's beautiful. She's… God, you have to *see* her." He let out a sigh. "She's confident and funny. Her work is… she's an amazing artist. There isn't anything she can't do."

"You've been watching her," I said, softening my voice. It was noble. It was what I would have done. I touched his hand back, 'It's okay now," I reassured him.

"She thinks I'm in Japan, teaching English." I shoved another bite into my mouth and watched Ronan cut his pancakes into perfect rectangles with remarkable politeness.

"That's some serial killer shit right there, Ronan."

"Ivy…" I knew what was coming next.

"Yeah, I lead a *Coven.* Weird, right?" I answered without hearing him ask.

"No, that explains a lot." Ronan smiled and raised his eyebrows. "You saw my ghost the moment you laid eyes on me."

I smiled. I did. He was *creepy.* Though.

"What about… *Amelie?*" He asked a question I hadn't expected.

"There's still a lot of darkness out there. It'll take time to clean it up. But Amelie Wyld?"

Ronan shuddered at her name.

"Just trust me when I say, Amelie won't be a problem."

"Should I be concerned?" Ronan asked as he placed one of his perfectly cut rectangles into his mouth.

I shook my head confidently. "So, what's next, Ro? Can I call you that? We're friends now, right?"

"I'll convince her to fall in love with me all over again."

That damn hopeful glint in his eyes was infectious.

I laughed and stood, grabbing my cloak. "That's ambitious. You know she's stubborn, right?"

I began walking toward the door and paused. I had almost forgotten the most important part.

"Oh, Ronan, one more thing." I scrunched my face up again. "Isolde... can—how do I say this? *See* out of the portrait." I winked at him, "Don't do anything I wouldn't do—*you know*—in front of the canvas while it's uncovered." I stepped closer to the door.

"Or maybe *do*? If you're into that sorta thing." I yelled as the bells chimed behind me on my way out.

♫ "Six Feet Under" – Billie Eilish

CHAPTER 27

For Lease

The building was quiet, save for the echo of footsteps across the hardwood floors. It had been meticulously restored to its former glory as a factory from the turn of the century. Every detail had been painstakingly considered. It felt like a labor of love, a dedication to a more regal time.

"Industrial and historic," I repeated, staring at the vaulted ceilings.

"Wren, *this place...* You're going to fall in love here. I can feel it."

Theo had a point. It was stunning: the exposed brick walls, the heavy iron beams, and the ceilings.

God, these ceilings. I thought to myself, memorizing every pattern and texture. I worried for just a moment about what something like this might cost. I was merely a photographer, not even this city's best one.

Not yet, at least.

A studio, a gallery like this—would elevate me to the top. It was prime real estate at two exceptionally busy cross streets with more foot traffic than Times Square. Okay, not exactly, but more than what I currently have.

I looked at Theo, anticipation in his eyes, an excitement I was eager to share.

I fidgeted in my long wool coat. It felt like it was shrinking the farther we walked into the building. I felt so small in such a large space.

We were meeting the owner, the person who had put so much attention and love into this building. We would lose this opportunity if he didn't like me or our business plan.

We entered the main room, which stretched for what felt like miles. Golden light beamed through the massive floor-to-ceiling windows.

I grabbed Theo's hand. "Oh my—God."

"Oh, I know... right?" he whispered.

I could see my photographs here, hung from wires on thick canvases, with light filtering in over them. I could see the faces of all those people I'd brought with me over these last few hard years.

I could envision our non-profit helping people and raising awareness—as if it were right there before me.

And then, I saw *him. Ronan.*

The man from the alley and the coffee shop stood at the far window, leaning against its brick brace, backlit like a shadow the sun could not swallow.

My heart raced and I could feel my pulse thudding against the sides of my head. The shrinking coat tightened around my chest. He's the owner? Seriously?

I blinked repeatedly, trying to recover or understand how the universe had become so accustomed to tricking me.

This was business—this was professional.

Except it wasn't at all. It was Ronan *again*.

I wish I could text Sam and Ivy.

"Ah, Mr. Arslane, perfect timing," Theo said, oblivious to the sudden shift in tension in the giant room. "Theo Ashford," he extended his hand toward him. "Glad to put a face to the name." He smiled, holding Ronan's hand in a display of masculinity.

"This is Wren Rivers—the photographer I've been telling you about."

Ronan's eyes lingered on me. He stepped forward and extended his hand to me as well. His grip was warm, steady, and too familiar for my comfort.

"A pleasure to meet you, Wren."

I raised an eyebrow. "Mr. Arslane." His name tasted like I'd said it a thousand times. "We meet again."

"Some might think you're following me, Ms. Rivers," he teased as he pulled back, and it immediately released the tension between us.

"Ah, great. You two know each other," Theo piped, smiling and glancing between us as we slowly stared each other down.

∗∗∗

I toured the space, with Ronan walking a few steps ahead while Theo—Mr. Ashford—filled the air with numbers, zoning regulations, and estimated building costs. I barely heard him. This was his department, not mine. I just took the photos. He was the numbers guy. That's why our business arrangement worked so well.

My focus kept redirecting itself to Ronan—his allure, his mystery. He was a work of art, and I wanted to photograph him— here. In this room, leaning so casually against the brick while the sun tried to ignite him.

I refrained from pulling out my camera.

***

I gave Theo a slight nod. I knew the cost would be significant. I'd have to make some cuts in other areas, but it was worth what we'd gain in return. This building would eventually pay for itself.

"Mr. Arslane," Theo approached him.

"Call me Ronan. Mr. Arslane was my father." Ronan smiled humbly.

"Ronan," Theo paused, "Wren and I, we'd love to be considered as your primary tenant, all twenty thousand square—"

Theo's phone suddenly buzzed, and his eyes widened with panic. It softened to an excited, tender stare.

"Wren, I have to go. I am so sorry." He apologized, "Emily's in labor. I'm having a baby!" He quickly backed toward the door, fumbling with his laptop bag.

"That's amazing, Theo—bring her my love!" I chuckled.

"Ronan will take care of you—you're in good hands!" He practically shouted it.

And then he was gone, leaving the room buzzing with excitement but enveloped in sudden silence. The sun faded behind the skyline of busy buildings, and the warm Edison bulbs cast only a subtle glow in the room.

"He's having a girl, he's been talking about her for nine months—without even existing yet, she's already the love of his life." I stared at the doorway he'd run through.

I am excited for my business partner and friend, but there was something I now needed to accomplish, far from my comfort zone. I didn't do real estate; I was the artist.

"What about you, Mr. Arslane?" I asked, breaking the tension. "Are there any children at home?"

He shook his head casually. "I'm not married, Ms. Rivers." He flashed a sly smile as he answered.

"So," I said, trying to keep it light, still. "This is a lovely place you have here."

He scanned the building, his smile shifting as if he had recalled something.

"Do you want to see how this place feels at night?" he asked, his voice a whisper, as the echo was startling.

I hesitated, then nodded. "Sure."

✳✳✳

We walked the length of the large room where I had first seen him. The city lights outside glared against the windows, blurring into a rainbow of colors that slowly twinkled. He was right. This place was even more beautiful at night.

I stared at the dark view and saw Ronan's reflection in the window. He moved slowly, like honey on a cold day. Yet, with each step he took, my pulse fired rapidly inside me.

As vast as it was, the room seemed to shrink with each heartbeat. Before I knew it, it was just him and me, and our world had melted away.

There was no room, no empty building.

Ronan turned toward me, his hand extended.

"Dance with me," he said.

I blinked. "There's no music."

He smiled softly. "We'll make our own."

His eyes were steady, his hand unwavering. It seemed he wouldn't take no for an answer. I placed my hand in his, and a spark of electricity snapped between our fingers.

"Oh," I flinched.

"A spark of magic." I was nervous, but I said it anyway.

He pulled me closer, his other hand settled gently on my waist.

We swayed slowly and intentionally, as if we had all the time in the world, and I felt caught in a moment that was too perfect for words.

"You *are* good at this," I whispered.

"I've had some practice." His voice cracked slightly.

I nearly laughed at how absurd it was—dancing with a near stranger in an empty building at night, with no music—but it felt natural despite its absurdity.

It felt like a memory.

My head rested on his shoulder, and for the first time in a long while, I felt safe. It felt as though I had discovered something—someone who had been missing.

"I'm sorry if this is forward, Mr. Arslane," I hesitated, uncertain why I had whispered it.

"Ronan," he corrected, his lips near my temple.

"Ronan," I said softly, tasting his name like a forbidden fruit that I'd much rather taste again.

And again.

He pulled back slightly, just enough to meet my gaze. His thumb brushed gently across my cheek, an innocent touch that sent a rush reverberating through me.

"It feels like I've known you forever," I sighed. "Do you think that's possible?"

He didn't answer right away.

"I do." His thumb hovered just above my lips, and I held my breath.

"Perhaps we knew each other in another life," he added softly, still staring deeply into my eyes.

I smiled, and my cheeks heated. "Do you believe in reincarnation?"

"Oh, certainly, Little Bird." His eyes fell to my mouth as he gently bit his lower lip.

"Do you think—" I paused, preparing to cross a line.

I had lived so much of my life on one side, the safe side. I never walked it or crossed over it, even when it felt right. I believed in reincarnation, and I believed—without a doubt—that I had met Ronan before. Perhaps we were once married... or star-crossed lovers. This felt like a redo, a memory playing out again, but I couldn't find the words for what I wanted to ask—until he did.

"Do I think I'd ravage you on our wedding night?" He paused, "And take your Father's dowry?"

He finished my exact thought with fewer words.

"I—How?—"

Without words, and as if neither of us could survive another moment without tearing apart whatever this feeling was growing... His lips melted into mine, and I remembered *this* mouth and *this* kiss. This was mine, *it was.*

My hands and fingers tangled in his hair as I gripped him harder, digging into him, afraid that if I let go, I would lose everything again.

I was afraid I'd forget again.

Our bodies collided with the brick, and his mouth met mine again, stealing every breath I gave to him. His teeth grazed my bottom lip, rattling me as I let out a low yelp.

His hands tightened around my waist, his fingertips digging into my hips, pressing me against the wall before pulling me back to him, closer—harder.

I gasped as his mouth moved down my neck, finding all of the small places that made my body arch with pleasure.

"Ronan—I—" My composure shatters as I lose the words I want to say.

He pulled back just long enough to look at me. Our eyes met, and I saw a familiar, feral, hungry look in his gaze. His thumb brushed over my lips again, and his voice was achingly beautiful— rough as if it had finally rested at the height of a mountain he'd climbed.

"This was us," He confessed, an admission that I'd been with him before. How could I not remember such violent, demanding passion? I felt at a disadvantage, this man knowing too many of my secrets and using them to unleash my wildest dreams.

Maybe it was another life.
Because if it were this one...
I'd remember this fire.
I'd remember this.

"Show me," I whispered, my fingers mercilessly gripping the controlled chaos of his body. It was a dare, a challenge, and it felt as if he had been waiting for me to say it his entire life.

And that was all it took—he surged back into me, lifting me effortlessly as my legs wrapped around his waist. His body pressed firmly into mine, every inch of his desire thrumming against me.

His mouth crashed impatiently against mine again, his hands shearing off my clothes, layer by layer, as anticipation built until he reached my skin.

I reached out and slowly unclasped every button on his loose-fitting shirt, tossing it away and letting it dance down to the ground, caught in the wind.

He generously ran his mouth down every inch that was available to him, pressing my body back into the stone, forcing his mouth deeper into the parts of me that wanted him.

"Ronan," I whispered breathlessly, the sound of his name lost in the night.

"Are you sure?" He whispered back.

"Never more," I said.

Ronan's laugh was radiant yet tragic, as if I had just told the world's cruelest—but most beautiful—joke ever.

Or like I'd said it before.

♫ "Stay" – Rihanna, Mikky Ekko

CHAPTER 28

Stay

Ronan Arslane, present day.

Ivy reassured me that the curse was gone. No lingering magic, no threads tying us back to the Badlands. Isolde was trapped. We were free. Wren was free.

I had made a promise that I couldn't keep, and it was tearing at me in a way that was unfamiliar. I had promised myself that I would show her and help Wren remember what we had. I was so sure it would be enough—enough for her to feel it again, to fall into me like she always had.

But after that night in the empty building, something inside me cracked. Guilt, a distinctly human emotion that I was still learning to carry, twisted in my chest.

Wren didn't remember me. Not the way I remembered her.

She didn't know the color of my eyes in the dim light of dawn. She couldn't recall how I touched her, how my fingers traced her lips before our first kiss. She didn't remember being my Little Bird.

But I did. Every gaze, every touch, every whispered word echoed in my mind. I was holding her life in my hands, manipulating fate itself by knowing all the right things to say, and all the perfect ways to make her fall.

I had become a magician without magic, using our history as a trick to pull her back to me.

It wasn't love; it was a trap—a spell without words. I was just as bad as Isolde, cursing Wren into a love she could not choose.

If Wren didn't choose me on her own—without me guiding her— then it isn't real. Not for her. Not for us.

I almost wished the curse had also taken my memory, so we could fall together, unburdened by what had broken us. If she couldn't remember me, then I would let her go.

Truly let her go.

So I did.

I sent a proxy to sign the lease. I chose to deal strictly with Mr. Ashford, keeping my distance. The pain of my decision cut far too deep for me to see her. I couldn't look into her eyes for the last time, knowing that her love for me had faded into nothing.

Knowing that Isolde had won, *yet again.*

After the dust had settled following my departure, I'd transfer full ownership of the building to her foundation in a few months. I'd walk away quietly, a ghost once again.

I stared at the wall in my simple apartment. Isolde's gruesome face looked out at me. I smiled at her and stepped closer to the frame, dragging my fingers over her crinkled skin.

"You wretched witch, you will have wished Ivy Holloway had given you the gift of death."

I tossed the velvet over the frame, and I left my apartment.

♫ "Gravity" – Sara Bareilles

CHAPTER 29

Memory

The gallery buzzed with life, alive with the chaos and excitement of a highly anticipated grand opening. The spotlights flickered on and off as the tech team worked to troubleshoot the issues. The catering company filled the air with the sweet, savory aroma of all my favorite comfort foods.

Crates of unused frames and tangled cabling lay scattered throughout the room, cluttering the vast space.

My head tilted ever so slightly, and I felt my eyebrow twitch under the pressure of uncertainty. Something was missing. I hand-selected every portrait in this room, each with its own story and a place close to my heart, and every one of them felt like they were where they belonged, but still... there was a void.

A deep thrumming of absence enveloped me, as I felt the weight of something important missing. It was like tugging at the threads of a memory I couldn't quite recall.

Each part of the exhibit was layered with pieces of my soul— or, at least, that's how it felt. I had poured everything I had into this room and these photos, and in just a few hours, I would let the world see all the different parts of me.

I'd let the world see who Wren Rivers *really* was.

Ivy gently placed her hand on my shoulder, letting me know she was here.

"Ah, just the person I was looking for." I smiled as I handed her a clipboard. "I need this place... cleaned up."

Ivy's eyes lit up with enthusiasm that tickled me. She loved telling people what to do, and it was always a good time when she did.

"But first," I said while hugging her. I hadn't seen her much since she returned from Japan. Three years felt like centuries because she was teaching in a remote area that prevented her from calling.

At all.

For three years, I'd scaled the walls of every possible bad thing that might have happened to her, down to the gory scent of metallic blood I'd conjured. But she rocked Sam and my world when she came fluttering into our café, a changed woman.

She returned fiercer than I'd ever seen her. She came back unleashed. Wild potential, relentless pursuit, and... bossing people around as if it were her day job.

And it was. When she returned, I'd asked Ivy to be my director of operations here at the gallery. It's temporary. I know better than to think I can keep an Ivy trapped in my gallery.

We both released our too-comfortable embrace and stared at the wall together. I could see her eyes darting over, waiting to ask—

"'Ey Wren?"

"Yes, Ivy..."

"Wha—uhh—what are we looking at?" It came out as one big long word.

"Something's missing. *Someone's missing*, I just—" I paused and sighed, "I don't know who it is," I joked.

"Ah, can I help?" She looked at me with a depth that could conceal no secrets.

"Maybe. Got any ideas on what might go there?" I gestured to the nearly eight-foot blank space.

"I just cleaned out your office." Her nose scrunched—that place was a disaster.

"And I found something that might help." She grinned. She was up to no good, and I could see the mischievous glint in her eyes.

We returned to the room, which was now spotless and meticulously organized.

"Now I won't know where anything is!" I teased.

"You didn't know where anything was before, Wren." She raised an eyebrow.

"*God*, I know, right?" I smiled and sat on the leather settee.

"Look!" She held up an old laptop.

"What is—" I stopped. "Oh my god, is that my laptop from after Evan?" I said his name without the slightest flinch.

"Yes—yes it is." She glared at me. "I thought..." She stopped.

"That it might have some of my best work on it," I finished her sentence.

"Maybe?" She squinted. "You high-tailed it so fast out of this city and moved hours away to a random town in a random state." Ivy recollected a chapter of my story that I so often forgot about.

"Sam and I barely know what your life was like then. You left us, and we were supportive, but—" she stopped.

"I thought maybe you'd like to try to remember what you were doing there in the first place." Her point finally landed.

"You know, Ivy," I picked at my nail, considering it. "It's not a bad idea." *I agreed.* That was when my heart was in limbo, where things weren't right, but I made a home for myself. I crawled away to a land of isolation, and maybe some of that darkness is the truth missing from this gallery.

Some of my demons *should* live here.

I opened the laptop and placed it on the edge of the desk. For a device I hadn't turned on in at least three years, the battery's full charge was miraculous.

There wasn't much, just a single folder, "Halethorpe."

I blinked at the name, wishing I'd felt a pang of regret or nostalgia, but I didn't. That time in my life felt more about survival than living. I double-clicked the folder, and a few hundred thumbnails materialized before me.

I glanced up at Ivy, who I knew was intently watching me while pretending to fiddle with paper on the other side of the desk. She was checking me for weaknesses or panic, but I remained steady.

Exploring my past didn't scare me anymore.

I clicked through some truly beautiful photographs: the old tree in the backyard with the tire swing, moody shots of the house in the cool winter light, and close-up shots showcasing the delicate ornate filigree of the mantle.

My breath caught at the sight of a shape, a *familiar* shape.

I clicked it open immediately, and it was exactly what I'd thought it was—a stunning portrait of Ronan Arslane.

It was unmistakably him or his twin. He stood centered in the shot, with dappled light and shadows framing his face in a way that made him seem otherworldly, like a phantom whose feet were planted in two different worlds.

I absorbed each detail, and the longer I observed it, the more I began to notice about it.

It felt intimate. He was shirtless, but the darkness obscured his details, revealing only the outline of his body. Had I ever been in a room with a shirtless Ronan before our night in this building?

Before the coffee?

I hadn't taken this photo. That wasn't possible.

My pulse pounded, shaking my adrenaline awake. My mind scattered abruptly, trying to make sense of such a world-shattering revelation. How could his photo have found its way into this folder on a laptop that I hadn't turned on in years?

The answer was plain and simple. It couldn't have.

"Oh my god," I whispered.

"Guess you found your someone," Ivy chimed, unable to see my screen.

"It's Ronan..."

Ivy knew everything about him. I couldn't contain the details of the night I'd spent with him here, the *generous* owner of this building.

"Na-uh," Ivy said, "You just met him. How—" Ivy's grin spread wildly across her face, and if I didn't know her any better, I'd say she might have done this.

"Oh, maybe he's in the cloud," Ivy suggested, her eyes lighting up as if she'd made a great discovery.

I tilted my head and raised my eyebrow, but wouldn't dare ask her if she had planted this. Maybe it wasn't Ronan. Maybe I had a one-night stand with a man strikingly similar to Ronan. But even if that was what it was—I wanted to tell this part of my story and remember the darkness.

These photos were likely some of my best work, and they belonged to me. This was my house, and the EXIF details indicated my camera.

Without hesitation, I sent the image to the printer. The benefit of having a space large enough was that all of my printing was now done in-house. I had my assistant fetch it, and when she returned, the sly grin on her face indicated that she, too, thought it was Ronan Arslane.

I found a simple black frame in the supply closet and carefully mounted it with a large black mat. I then hung it in the center of the feature wall.

It truly was an incredible image.

And I was going to find out where it came from.

***

I hadn't seen or talked to Ronan since the night when things spiraled out of control in this building. I think the gravity of what we'd experienced had frightened him slightly.

He sent a proxy to sign the lease documents and requested to deal strictly with Theo. At that time, I had told myself it wasn't me.

Me: Come to the gallery. There's something I need you to see.

I watched the dots of a reply appear and disappear, but nothing came to confirm his attendance.

***

The door creaked open, and Ronan stepped inside, his silhouette framed by the soft light of the dim gallery spotlights. He walked toward me with his usual grace, but there was something different this time—a distance.

"What's so urgent, Ms. Rivers?" he asked, his voice polite but cold.

Ms. Rivers?

The formality of his tone stung, cutting through the memory of our last night here—the passion and the breathless urgency that had left us tangled on the floor, consumed by each other.

Now, he looked at me like a stranger.

"Wh—why are you being like this? I asked, my voice steady despite the crashing pain radiating inside me. "You're just going to pretend that we didn't happen?" I asked, regaining my confidence.

"Are you ashamed?" I hadn't given him a moment's grace.

"Wh—No. Ms. Rivers," he shook his head in confusion. "I just think we should maintain a professional relationship." His answer stung, but it felt empty, like even he didn't believe it. I'd known liars. I knew lies. Ronan Arslane wasn't a liar, and he was lying through his teeth.

"Well then, Mr. Arslane," I let his name roll off my tongue in my most professional voice as I gestured toward the feature wall. His gaze followed my hand, and the moment his eyes landed on the portrait, his entire body tensed.

"It is rather curious, though, Mr. Arslane," my tone still high-pitched with harmonic professionalism, "that despite your desire for our professionalism, you keep finding yourself half-dressed in my life." I was calm, cool confidence as I revealed what had been tattering my mind, fraying it at the ends with confusion.

"Where did you get that?" He whispered, almost to himself.

"Why don't you tell me?" I crossed my arms, trying to steady my racing heart. I stepped toward him, refusing to let him slip back into the shadows.

"What were you doing in Halethorpe? Why do I have a photo of you that I don't remember taking?"

His jaw tightened. Perhaps he realized this was a trap. He would finally be forced to provide some real answers, but as the moment stretched, I thought he might run.

"You're hiding something. I know it. You've been distant since the night we—" I stopped, heat rushing to my face; my cheeks flushed.

"Since the night you made me believe in something," I took a deep breath, "And now?" I paused. "You're here, pretending it never happened?

I breathed heavier than I had thought, forcing back tears that threatened to escape. I wouldn't let them. I wouldn't crack.

"It's not that simple, Wren," he snapped, his eyes dark.

"You say my name like you've said it a thousand times before," I whispered.

"You think I don't want to stay? You think I don't—" He stopped, his chest rising and falling with heavy, deep breaths. "You think I don't live in that memory every minute, of every day?"

"What are you afraid of? I stepped closer to him, and he moved away.

He hesitated, his eyes darting between mine. His breathing became shallow, and his body tensed.

"I'm afraid..." His voice dropped lower as he made this admission.

"I'm afraid you'll fall in love with me because I'll lead you there. Because I'll say all the right things. Because I'll know exactly how to make you feel safe and wanted." He stopped, his chest rising and falling with deep, deliberate breaths.

"I'm afraid it won't be real—not for you."

The words settled, landing heavy and raw.

I blinked, trying to make sense of what he was saying. "You think you can manipulate me into loving you?" My voice was softer now, filled with curiosity.

"I don't *think*," he whispered, "I know I could," his eyes torn with conflict. "But how could I not? Every time I look at you, I remember all the pieces of us you've forgotten. And I want to give them back to you. I want to pull you into them, remind you of everything we were."

He ran a hand through his hair, feeling frustrated and broken. "But it wouldn't be your choice. Not really. It would be mine."

"Ronan—"

"You deserve the kind of love that's free, wild, and entirely your own. Not something crafted by someone who already knows the ending."

I swallowed, my throat dry and sore.

"I don't care how it started," I said, stepping closer. He didn't move this time. "I care about how it feels right now. Here. With you."

I noticed his eyes soften when I realized what I'd just said. I reached for his hand and wove my fingers into his.

"You know me?" I asked gently, my voice too soft to echo.

He nodded silently, our eyes connecting.

"Better than anyone else ever has?" I arched my eyebrow at him as I questioned him. He nodded again, his eyes still locked on mine as he bit his lip slightly, as if he wanted to explode with all he knew, to tell me every secret he'd memorized.

"You have seen me at my best and worst?" I questioned.

He nodded and smiled slightly. He started, "I've seen your hair after a reckless weekend rotting in bed," he teased. "A mess."

I smiled back, and I saw something familiar. He hadn't been lying. I knew this man... I felt it in parts of my soul that I shouldn't.

"And you still look at me like I'm something worth loving?" I paused, compelling him to meet my eyes with his again.

"Why are you so afraid of giving me the chance to love you back?"

"Wren—" he groaned, squeezing my hand with his.

"So what if I can't remember everything? I know how I feel when I'm with you, and—" I stopped and caught my breath.

"I'm choosing that. I'm choosing you." I was demanding that he accept me.

He sighed. It was a mix of relief and concession. The fight faded from his eyes, and he asked, "Are you sure?"

"Never more," I said softly, without even thinking.

His eyes widened slightly. "You've said that twice now, do you remember it?"

I blinked, a wave of embarrassment flushing my cheeks, "I—I don't. It just... felt right."

Our hands tightened around each other's, fingers interlaced.

"Stay," I whispered.

♫ "Turning Page" – Sleeping At Last

CHAPTER 30

The End

The grand opening was a tremendous success. Both prints and originals sold en masse. The press, in all its forms, infiltrated the first few hours but gradually stepped back and joined the celebration off the record.

Champagne glasses clinked, and a soft melody drifted from the soulful singer, who strummed his guitar and sang like a man with a shattered heart.

I stood near the bar with Ivy and Sam, taking it all in, finding the night and everything we had accomplished unbelievable.

"You really did it, Wren," Ivy said, giving me a sideways hug. "I always knew you were something special. This is… It's perfect."

"And the lighting makes me look flawless, which is the most important part," Sam added, striking a dramatic pose under one of the Edison bulbs.

I rolled my eyes and sipped the bubbly champagne in my glass. "Of course, I put that there just for you."

"Speaking of flawless..." Sam said, nearly out of breath from his acrobatics, "Where's your mysterious guest? Mr. Tall, Dark, and Broody?"

"*Sam!*" Ivy warned, slapping the back of her hand against Sam's chest.

"This lighting, *that* singer, this gallery... It's like we're stuck in a Katherine Heigl movie and can't get out."

I started to reply, but the music shifted to something softer. The tempo slowed, and the familiar melody sent electricity down my spine. My body tensed as if it knew it was supposed to be doing something that it wasn't.

And there he was.

Ronan.

He moved through the crowd; our eyes met, and he cracked a smile. He stopped just a few feet from where I stood and extended his hand.

"Dance with me?"

My heart leapt, thudding away as if it had missed a few beats. I glanced between Sam and Ivy; both nodded, as if to say, 'What are you waiting for?'

I intertwined my fingers with Ronan's, and he drew me close, pressing himself against me. I melted into his embrace as the lyrics lingered in my ears, a story about time that tickled my soul.

"You know, Little Bird, this is how we once said goodbye," he whispered into my ear as we swayed in time with the beat.

I smiled softly. He knew I couldn't remember, but I was aware that he did. It wasn't just my body urging me to dance; it was the shadow of my memories, aching for me to recall.

"Then, let's make this time forever," I said as I lay my head comfortably on his chest, letting his heartbeat mingle with the melody—a love song just for me.

His hand rested at the small of my back, and we continued to sway, moving in together as if we had done this a thousand times before tonight.

"I really do feel like I've known you forever," I said, the music muffling much of what I had said.

Ronan's thumb brushed over the back of my hand. "Some souls are meant to find each other, no matter what." My heart fluttered as I considered the magic and hope behind such a thought.

✳✳✳

From across the room, Ivy nudged Sam. "Did you see that? Now, *that's* a grand romantic gesture." She smiled.

Sam nodded, his eyes sparkling with happiness as he watched his best friend fall in love on the dance floor. "Six months. Max."

"Three," Ivy replied, slurping her drink and grinning.

"If they don't have an open bar, I'm not officiating—" Sam replied.

Ivy abruptly replied, "Uhh, Sam?"

"Yes, V?"

"I think you have an admirer." Ivy gestured to one of the guitar players standing on the other side of the bar. "He's been eyeing you all night."

Sam's cheeks blushed. "Well, then, let's not keep the man waiting. The love of his life just arrived."

***

In the final moment of our dance, I realized that some stories are meant to be told twice.

♫ "Lights On" – H.E.R.

BONUS

Isolde

Ronan and I barely made it through the door before we were tangled on the living room floor—clothes lost along the way and our bodies pressed into the cloud-soft carpet.

With the taste of champagne and bourbon on our lips, we slowly undid one another, piece by piece, kiss by kiss. My mouth traveled the lines of his body, and his hands traced the curves of mine. We tantalized each other until nothing was left, and then the fun began.

As I broke free from the hold of the moment, I approached the side bar and poured myself a drink from something ancient—a prized possession of my mysterious lover.

He positioned himself behind me, pressing against me as a reminder that we were not yet finished with what we had started. I sipped the amber potion, which burned with a fruited tang. Across the room, a painting—a portrait—caught my eye.

Covered by a massive velvet sheet.

"Ronan?"

He hummed a tune while sliding his mouth along my neck, shoulders, and back.

"What's that?" I asked, curiously staring at the dark mass.

"What's what?" He finally pulled away from me and looked toward where my gaze was locked.

"Ah, that's… Isolde." He answered, taking the cup from my hand and pressing it to his lips.

"Isolde?" I asked again, feeling left behind without my memories. "I should know her?"

"Yes and no, but she is of no matter at this moment," Ronan said. He returned the glass and turned me to face him, retracting my gaze and pulling my mouth toward his. I could taste the bourbon on him, letting it burn through our kiss.

He cupped my face and ran his hands back through my hair, which felt comforting, but…

"Who is she?" I interrupted again.

Ronan sighed but smiled. He was gentle with all that I had forgotten. He tucked my hair behind my ear and leaned back against the counter. His body was fully displayed, unashamed of how ready he was.

"Isolde is the witch who cursed me—" He paused. "*Us.*" He glanced toward the space where the painting was concealed.

"She's… alive?" I felt concerned and scared. "Why is she—why do you have her here?"

"A powerful witch trapped her in the painting that once held me," Ronan said, blinking and staring blankly at Isolde.

"She's trapped for an eternity, but…" He paused. "She can *see.*"

My eyes widened. "She can see... out of the painting?" I questioned. My body tensed. Ronan's hand ran down my side, stopping at the small of my back and pulling me into him.

"Wh—who put her in that painting?"

Ronan's eyes winced, and he hesitated momentarily, as if he were afraid of the answer. "A story for another day," he whispered into my ear, letting my fear slide off my body.

"You have nothing to worry about. That's why she's covered." Ronan reassured me, his gaze firm and unwavering. I trusted him.

I glanced back at Isolde.

"She cursed us?" I asked again.

"Yes, me in the painting for five hundred years, as her ward." He said, "And you, when she took your memories in exchange for my release."

"She kept you for five hundred years?" I said softly, "In a painting?"

"Well, in a reality of her design, I was forced to fulfill whatever deeds she required of me." He hesitated, afraid to fully reveal what had happened to him.

"She forced you?" I said, reaching out to console him. He smirked with one side of his mouth. "My mind was stronger than her broken false realities, Little Bird."

"Ronan—" I said, brushing my hand along his face.

"I have an idea." I crinkled my nose. "Do you trust me?" A devilish grin slid across my face.

"Always."

"Take the sheet off of her." I requested.

Ronan's expression turned serious as he approached her painting, growing slightly concerned, but he did not ask why or question me.

"She's... hideous and rather frightening," he called out, his back turned toward me as he walked toward her.

"Good," I said.

When Ronan dropped the velvet from the painting, the room shifted, and the air twisted slightly. The feeling of being watched wasn't just paranoia—it was real. Isolde's frozen scream widened, and her eyes became dark pools of rage and despair—a grim reminder of everything we'd survived.

And yet—she *saw*.

Unblinking, she was unable to hide from anything she feared. Unable to ever *not* see that which made the world turn.

I had hoped her face might trigger my memories. I thought maybe I would recognize her, but I didn't. Unlike when I had seen Ronan, there wasn't even a hint of recognition in her features. Perhaps she looked different before.

But now, she was nothing more than an ugly stranger with no meaning.

I walked over to her and traced my finger along the soft paint.

Ronan had already retreated to our spot on the floor, instantly turning his back to her as if he still recoiled from her aura.

I stared into her eyes. They looked real but were painted. I could feel her thrumming inside, how irritated her soul had become. I wondered if she could ever escape, and if she could...

Would she come for me? Would she come for Ronan? Or would she fear whatever we had done to her and cower and run?

I leaned closer to the painting, my face nearly touching the dried oil inks mounded onto the ancient canvas. "Remember me?" I whispered so Ronan couldn't hear me.

"I hope you like the view, Isolde," I whispered, my breath brushing against the canvas.

"Every kiss, every gasp, every deep moan of pleasure. You'll have nothing but the jealousy that trapped you there to keep you company," I whispered.

"I won."

Ronan, who had just finished the last of the bourbon, was half sprawled on the floor, waiting patiently for my return.

"Leave it off," I straddled him. "I want her to *remember* what she lost."

PLAYLIST

Available on Spotify

Aly Anders has curated this playlist to represent the story of The Art of a Curse—each song recreating the feeling of the chapters as an "after it's over" experience. There is no intent for these to be listened to at the same time as you are reading, and it is not meant to replace any of the feelings you would get from the retelling of Wren and Ronan's love story.

"Can't Pretend" – Tom Odell
"I Found" – Amber Run
"Creep – Acoustic" – Radiohead
"Trouble" – Valerie Broussard
"Hands To Myself" – Selena Gomez
"Take Me To Church" – Hozier
"everything sucks" – vaultboy
"WITHOUT YOU" – The Kid LAROI
"Omens" – UNSECRET, Neoni
"River" – Bishop Briggs
"Dangerous Woman" – Ariana Grande
"Bad Intentions" – Niykee Heaton
"Rivers & Roads" – The Head & The Heart
"Time After Time" – Tyler Ward
"I See Red" – Everybody Loves an Outlaw
"Heart of Darkness" – Steelfeather

"Gasoline" – Halsey
"Can't Fight" – Lianne La Havas
"golden hour" – JVKE
"Beautiful Things" – Benson Boone
"Back from the Fire" – Gold Brother
"Lost Without You" – Freya Ridings
"Beyond" – Leon Bridges
"Vigilante Shit" – Taylor Swift
"Rise Up" – Andra Day
"Six Feet Under" – Billie Eilish
"Electric" – Alina Baraz, Khalid
"Stay" – Rihanna, Mikky Ekko
"Gravity" – Sara Bareilles
"Turning Page" – Sleeping At Last
"Lights On" – H.E.R

THE HALETHORPE CHRONICLES

A Literary Gothic Series of Obsession, Haunting, and Fate.

Some places never let go.
Some souls refuse to be forgotten.
And some stories are meant to be told twice.

Welcome to **Halethorpe**, a town where the past lingers in the shadows, the dead leave their mark on the living, and the walls whisper secrets to those who dare to listen. Beneath its fading grandeur, Halethorpe pulses with something darker—a thread of magic, madness, and memory that entangles those who seek truth in its ruins.

Each novel in *The Halethorpe Chronicles* is a standalone gothic tale, weaving together cursed legacies, supernatural forces, and the aching pull of love lost and found again.

Aly Anders dives deep into the heart of humanity, telling stories deeply connected to facing the things that hurt you, refusing to be controlled by them, and learning that even if you lose pieces of yourself along the way, the things that matter—love, resilience, and the parts of who you once were—can never be truly erased.

ACKNOWLEDGEMENTS

Thank you & Dedications

Will... You let me black out and write this in two weeks. Thank you for handling our lives while I disappeared. Being married to me can't be easy, but you make it look like it is. I love you with everything I am.

Wren Rivers, you remind me of myself in so many ways, maybe because I invented you from parts and pieces of me that were broken by years of poorly designed men. I am glad that I wrote you a happy ending.

Maddie P. for being the first reader of every story I write.

Jess P. for helping me turn a suspect carrom board into this story.

And all my friends and family for not judging me while they read some of my more intimate writing.

Anyone who reads this story, or any of the Halethorpe Chronicles installments. *Thank you for your time and commitment.*

Supporting independent authors is a special cause for which we are endlessly thankful. If you loved what you read, consider leaving a review. It's free to tell others how much you enjoyed this story.

www.ingramcontent.com/pod-product-compliance
Lightning Source LLC
Chambersburg PA
CBHW031426200626
46814CB00016B/2379